Penguin Books
Daughters of Passion

Julia O'Faolain was born in London, brought up in Dublin, educated in Rome and Paris and married in Florence to an American historian, Lauro Martines. After living for several years in Florence, interrupted by a spell in Oregon, Professor Martines took a job at UCLA, and they now commute between London and Los Angeles. Julia O'Faolain has worked as a teacher (of languages and interpreting) and as a translator. Her books include *Women in the Wall* (1978, Penguin), *No Country For Young Men* (1980, Penguin), which was shortlisted for the Booker McConnell Prize of that year, and *The Obedient Wife* (1982).

Daughters of Passion

stories by **Julia O'Faolain**

For Dick and Mary

with love,

Julia O'Faolain

16 November, 1982.

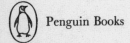 Penguin Books

Penguin Books Ltd, Harmondsworth, Middlesex, England
Penguin Books, 625 Madison Avenue, New York, New York 10022, U.S.A.
Penguin Books Australia Ltd, Ringwood, Victoria, Australia
Penguin Books Canada Ltd, 2801 John Street, Markham, Ontario, Canada L3R 1B4
Penguin Books (N.Z.) Ltd, 182–190 Wairau Road, Auckland 10, New Zealand

Legend for a Painting first published in *Cosmopolitan* (USA) 1976
The Nanny and the Antique Dealer first published in the *New Review* 1976
Daughters of Passion first published in the *Hudson Review* 1980
Oh My Monsters: first published in the *New Review* 1976
Mad Marga first published in *Triquarterly* 50 1981
Why Should Not Old Men Be Mad? first published in *Winter's Tales* 26 1981
Will You Please Go Now first published in *Company* magazine 1981
Bought first published (under a different title) in the *New Review* 1977

This collection first published in Penguin Books 1982

Made and printed in Great Britain by
Richard Clay (The Chaucer Press) Ltd, Bungay, Suffolk
Set in Monophoto Baskerville

Contents

Legend for a Painting 9

The Nanny and the Antique Dealer 12

Daughters of Passion 39

Oh My Monsters! 62

Mad Marga 85

Why Should Not Old Men Be Mad? 100

Will You Please Go Now 124

Bought 136

Diego 151

For Eileen

Legend for a Painting

A knight rode to a place where a lady was living with a dragon. She was a gently bred creature with a high forehead, and her dress – allowing for her surroundings – was neat. While the dragon slept, the knight had a chance to present himself.

'I have come,' he told the lady, 'to set you free.' He pointed at a stout chain linking her to her monstrous companion. It had a greenish tinge, due the knight supposed to some canker oozing from the creature's flesh.

Green was the dragon's colour. Its tail was green; so were its wings, with the exception of the pale pink eyes which were embedded in them and which glowed like water-lilies and expanded when the dragon flew, as eyes do on the spread tails of peacocks. Greenest of all was the dragon's under-belly which swelled like sod on a fresh grave. It was heaving just now and emitting gurgles. The knight shuddered.

'What,' the lady wondered, 'do you mean by "free"?'

The knight spelled it: 'F-R-E-E', although he was unsure whether or not she might be literate. 'To go!' he gasped for he was grappling with distress.

'But where?' the lady insisted. 'I like it here, you know. Draggie and I' – the knight feared her grin might be mischievous or even mad – 'have a perfect symbiotic relationship!'

The knight guessed at obscenities.

'I clean his scales,' she said, 'and he prepares my food. We have no cutlery so he chews it while it cooks in the fire from his throat: a labour-saving device. He can do rabbit stew, braised wood pigeon, even liver Venetian style when we can get a liver.'

9

'God's blood!' the knight managed to swear. His breath had been taken away.

'I don't know that recipe. Is it good? I can see,' the lady wisely soothed, 'you don't approve. But remember that fire scours. His mouth is germ free. Cleaner than mine or your own, which, if I may say so with respect, has been breathing too close. Have you perhaps been chewing wild garlic?'

The knight crossed himself. 'You,' he told the lady, 'must be losing your wits as a result of living with this carnal beast!' He sprinkled her with a little sacred dust from a pouch that he carried about his person. He had gathered it on the grave of Saint George the Dragon Killer and trusted in its curative properties. 'God grant,' he prayed, 'you don't lose your soul as well. Haven't you heard that if a single drop of dragon's blood falls on the mildest man or maid, they grow as carnal as the beast itself? Concupiscent!' he hissed persuasively. 'Bloody! Fierce!'

The lady sighed. 'Blood does obsess you!' she remarked. 'Draggie never bleeds. You needn't worry. His skin's prime quality. Very resistant and I care for him well. He may be "carnal" as you say. We're certainly both carnivores. I take it you're a vegetarian?'

The knight glanced at the cankered chain and groaned. 'You're mad!' he ground his teeth. 'Your sense of values has been perverted. The fact that you can't see it proves it!'

'A tautology, I think?' The lady grinned. 'Why don't you have a talk with old Draggie when he wakes up? You'll see how gentle he can be. That might dispel your prejudices.'

But the knight had heard enough. He neither liked long words nor thought them proper in a woman's mouth. *Deeds not words* was the motto emblazoned on his shield, for he liked words that condemned words and this, as the lady could have told him, revealed inner contradictions likely to lead to trouble in the long run.

'Enough!' he yelled and, lifting his lance, plunged it several times between the dragon's scales. He had no difficulty in doing this, for the dragon was a slow-witted, somnolent beast at best and just now deep in a private dragon-dream. Its eyes, when they opened, were iridescent and flamed in the sunlight, turning, when the creature wept, into great, concentric, rainbow wheels of fire. 'Take that!' the knight was howling gleefully, 'and that and that!'

Blood spurted, gushed, and spattered until his face, his polished armour and the white coat of his charger were veined and flecked like porphyry. The dragon was soon dead but the knight's rage seemed unstoppable. For minutes, as though battening on its own release, it continued to discharge as he hacked at the unresisting carcass. Butchering, his sword swirled and slammed. His teeth gnashed. Saliva flowed in stringy beardlets from his chin and the lady stared at him with horror. She had been pale before but now her cheeks seemed to have gathered sour, greenish reflections into their brimming hollows.

Abruptly, she dropped the chain. Its clank, as it hit a stone, interrupted the knight's frenzy. As though just awakened, he turned dull eyes to her. Questioning.

'Then,' slowly grasping what this meant, 'you were never his prisoner, after all?'

The lady pointed at a gold collar encircling the dragon's neck. It had been concealed by an overlap of scales but had slipped into view during the fight. One end of the chain was fastened to it.

'He was mine,' she said. 'But as I told you he was gentle and more a pet than a prisoner.'

The knight wiped his eyelids which were fringed with red. He looked at his hands.

'Blood!' he shrieked. 'Dragon's blood!'

'Yes,' she said in a cold, taut voice, 'you're bloody. Concupiscent, no doubt? Fierce, certainly! Carnal?' She kicked the chain, which had broken when she threw it down and, bending, picked up a link that had become detached. 'I'll wear this,' she said bitterly, 'in token of my servitude. I'm your prisoner now.' She slipped the gold, green-tinged metal ring on to the third finger of her left hand. It too was stained with blood.

The Nanny and the Antique Dealer

'*Brutta!*'

The man raced off. The stuff of his mac wheezed. His hands were sly in its pockets. Bunched into fists, they held what? A gun? Money? His own balls? Elbows jutted behind him like amputated wings.

'*Brutta! Quanto sei brutta tu!*'

He was gone. Licketysplit around a dog-defaced corner.

Hanna tried to gauge the vibrancy surviving on wet air. *Brutta?* In nursery-Italian – she was here as a nanny – the word meant 'naughty'. Naughty nanny? She could have coped with that. She looked along forlorn pavements and came to a decision. She would offer herself a treat in one of those steamy bars which reminded her of bathrooms. They were full of glass, chrome and soapy smells like lime, camomile, anise.

'Gin,' she said, '*inglese,*' and laid her money out.

The expense was ruinous, but she needed the comfort. '*Brutta*' when you were not nine but twenty-nine meant 'ugly'.

The gin exploded in her chest like a firework. So did the insult. She could feel it warp her smile and humble her shoulders. Under the table her legs wove together like mutually supportive vines. Bravely she straightened them and faced into a mirror.

'Have sense,' she admonished it. 'Sticks and stones . . .'

She had been a nanny for scarcely a month but had already picked up nannyish turns of phrase. That was her trouble. She was open to persuasion. Silly really. At twenty-nine. But there you were: she was malleable. Open. This felt odd because until recently she had been someone quite opaque and solid. Until three months ago when Mummy died. She'd lived ten years with Mummy, taking care of her, making decisions, passing the time of day with neighbours who invited her over from kindness and because they knew she hadn't much of a life. The kindness prevented her knowing whether they'd maybe have liked her company anyway.

'Hullo Hanna,' they said when she came out to walk the dog or buy an evening paper. 'How's your mother?'

'Much the same, thanks.' Mummy had been an invalid.

'Drop by on Sunday if you'd like to take a hand at cards.'

Opaque. Solid. Not that she'd thought of it that way then. But now – she knew with a touch of sluggish excitement – she was different. Now people's thoughts could reach inside her just as a fly or crumb or drop of angostura could fall into and colour this glass of gin. She took a sip and enjoyed the blaze on her lips. Neat. She didn't like the taste but did the crude vigour of the stuff. Crude and powerful experiences awaited her, she knew. She had taken the post as nanny with this in mind. A nanny, in a villa in Italy far from home and protective gossip, must attract assault. She wanted this.

Hanna and Mummy, curled like cats before the television, two women waiting, one to die the other to live, had had time in their ten years together to dream and dissect the arithmetic of dream. Figuring with it, they agreed that Hanna's dutiful daughterliness would be rewarded, that her life with Mummy was a prelude, just as school had been, and that later she must change into something and someone quite unforeseen. 'Like a butterfly,' said Mummy who tended to be romantic. Why not? This fantasy future was for her vicarious. On Hanna it ended by imposing responsibilities.

After the funeral, offers had been made by relatives who supposed Hanna to be at a loss and in need of a breathing-time for finding her feet. She refused, answered an ad in *The Times* for a nanny needed by an English family in Tuscany, let Mummy's house, stored her things and came away with only a suitcase. In it were serviceable clothes and in her head secret, frankly rakish plans. These were simple. She would go where she would be a stranger. It was to strangers, she and Mummy had observed, that things happened. Not to the girl next door. And when something started to happen, Hanna would let it. She would do this for them both: the two who had waited, instruments tuned but unplayed for ten years.

All that time they had resounded inwardly, knowing themselves to be different from their neighbours whose fancy was dulled by school-reports, bills, recipes for stretching the Sunday joint. No question about it: Hanna and Mummy were as different from the others as chalk was from cheese. Day-glo chalk for drawing wild designs. They believed in passion, in privileged moments and the world well lost for one marvellous memory. To be sure, Mummy, whose own husband, Hanna's father, had been killed in Korea weeks after their honeymoon, was romancing backwards as well as forwards. Hanna could see that. But by the time she'd grown old enough to see it she could only see through the lens of an imagination dyed in her mother's colours: Madame Butterfly colours, iridescent, fast and doomed. Men, to appeal to Mummy, had to be Pinkertons. She had discouraged some local fellows who didn't fill her bill but might, given a chance, have started courting Hanna. Or so Hanna thought in retrospect. But couldn't be sure. She might be deceiving herself. Maybe they hadn't fancied her after all? She didn't understand people easily, had no idea how to flirt. She had no experience, was too much of a dreamer.

So was the man who had just insulted her. She'd recognized the yearning in him. His quick slither towards her showed he had recognized hers. She was a possible partner whom he had chosen to reject. Brutally. Why?

'*Brutta!*'

They'd said it to her before. Here in Poggibonsi and also in the village where she went to buy Kleenex, Tampax and English paperbacks, men had slid past her whispering intimate insults. Usually they wore trenchcoats: great rubberized affairs bristling with flaps which recalled Kurt Jurgens straddling decks or tanks and no doubt separated intimate wetnesses from the more general November damp. Yes, these were dreamers but had no place for her aboard their dream boats.

Too ugly? *Was* she? It had never occurred to her to wonder. Had it to Mummy? Hanna licked the edge of her gin glass and, leaving the bar, trudged back to the villa and up its drive at a humiliated lope. In the hall she pulled off muddy wellingtons and walked over to stare at herself in a mirror. Mirror, mirror – but it was leaden, tarnished, an antique. Besides, all fables tell and every nanny knows that frogs like frogs and dwarves have a gigantic opinion of themselves. Putting on her slippers, she went up to the nursery where she consoled herself in a game of Snap with Jane and Jeremy whom she had contracted to look after for at least six months. It had been on these terms that their parents had agreed to pay her fare from Dublin.

'Wouldn't you like to go into Florence, Hanna? We could give you a lift. It must be boring for you around here?'

Mrs Carr had lost one nanny already and was determined to hold on to Hanna. 'No,' said Hanna, 'thank you. I have a lot of letters to write.'

'Are you quite sure? It would be no trouble.'

In the end, as she couldn't go on refusing, she said 'yes'. She had already refused their offers to introduce her to other English-speaking girls. She was shy, knowing herself to be ten years behind her contemporaries, not to say twenty, considering that she'd been sent to a convent boarding school at the age of eight. That too had been an incubator for fancy: a fallow, moist estate full of rushes, willows and waterproof statues of the Virgin. Hanna had been one of the smartest pupils, graduating with First Class Honours in Gospel, Gaelic, Thomistic Logic, Church History and the History of Ireland.

The Carrs bickered all the way into Florence, their chins pitched at an identical, petulant tilt. They shared the same brand of good looks. Probably either could have driven the man who had insulted Hanna into a state of gibbering lust. Not that the Carrs would have noticed. They were a chilly pair, Hanna thought. Kind, certainly, but kindness could be an insulator. Probably her inquisitiveness had put them off. She couldn't control it. They were the first couple she had seen from close up and she was fascinated by their warmth, their coolness and the way they could rise from apparent boredom to fight or make love. She had steered the children from a hayloft where they had been at it one afternoon and, on another, overheard them in the bath which was late nineteenth-century and vast, with swans' necks looped like nooses in bas relief down sides propped on iron-webbed swans' feet.

'What,' Mr Carr had been whispering through a spittle of tap water, 'if I drowned you? Bitch.'

She had answered 'do' in a beseeching voice and Hanna,

experiencing their intimacy like a slap of steam, had felt her loneliness the more.

'We'll be leaving at six,' Mrs Carr told her. 'Where shall we meet?'

Hanna chose the teashop in the Piazza della Signoria. English people went there and she wouldn't stick out. The Carrs were two hours late but she waited as she couldn't think what else to do. It was lucky she had a book.

At eight o'clock Mr Carr rushed in. His face was wet and his eyes red.

'Oh so you're here,' he said as though surprised. 'Hurry, I'm triple-parked in the piazza.'

Hanna had to retrieve her umbrella and coat and by the time she reached the Mercedes, Mr Carr had it in gear.

'My wife has left me,' he said and began to cry. 'I thought she'd come back. But she didn't. She flew from Pisa. She has a lover,' he added and slammed his foot on the brake to avoid a pedestrian. A car bumped into the back of theirs and Hanna, thrown forward, hit her forehead against the windscreen. 'Oh bugger everything.' Mr Carr lowered his head on the steering-wheel.

Hanna managed to ease him out of the driving seat, sit in it herself and drive him home. When they reached the villa the cook had gone to bed. Beans, left warming on the stove, had burned and lamb chops shrivelled.

'I'll fry some eggs,' Hanna offered and did.

Mr Carr prodded them with his fork. The yolks shook. 'Do you know who she's gone to?' he asked Hanna. 'My wife. Elio. Can you imagine?'

Elio had been a guest at the villa up to a fortnight before.

'Ghastly twit,' said Mr Carr.

'More wine?' Hanna poured some.

Elio had been in Tuscany looking for antiques and had gone for long drives with Mrs Carr to see what they might find in out-of-the-way villas whose owners might not know the value of what they had. He had stayed about ten days.

'A scavenger,' stated Mr Carr. He finished his eggs quickly, wiped his mouth and eyes. 'I'm going to bed.'

'I'll lock up then.'

'Thanks.' He stood up and made unsteadily for the door. He looked as brittle as celery. Hanna could see suddenly that his wife might have been drawn to the assertive little intruder who had apparently winkled her out as easily as he had got village priests to sell him Church chattels with which they had no right to part since, strictly speaking, they were the property of the Italian State. Shady, she had thought at the time and she had been right.

Elio had been 'Elio' to everyone because, as he said himself, his surname, being Sephardic-Spanish, was unpronounceable. He was from North Africa, Jewish, now lived in Paris. He loved to explain: 'My people lived in North Africa for four hundred years. Ever since they were thrown out of Spain by Isabella. Now I have been eased out by the Algerians.'

'You did all right,' said Mrs Carr. 'Got out with a lot. He has a marvellous shop,' she told Hanna, 'in the rue de Seine.'

'They confiscated my library,' Elio complained.

'Erotica. Don't worry. It will corrupt them and avenge you.'

Mr Carr hadn't seemed to mind his wife's teasing this man whom he himself had hardly seemed to know. Perhaps he thought Elio too ugly to be a sexual threat? Or too much of a chatterbox? Elio was always offering himself for the company's amusement, telling stories, singing for his supper.

'I learned about women,' he said with his self-mocking shrug, 'from my mother. The usual story: she was beautiful, demanding, a bit of a bore. A woman of the old school. All ruffles.' He twitched his wrists in mimicry. 'She treated me like a lover when I was ten. My father never married or took responsibility for her. So I am, of course, a bastard. In law a bastard is entirely the mother's responsibility and she ends up in turn being his. Perhaps it's as well she died . . . I am so faithless.'

He was smooth, amphibious-looking. His skin gleamed. Like the dolphins in the villa fountains, he was over-streamlined. His shoulders especially seemed to have been eroded. The prominent belly, pulling his centre of gravity hipward, emphasized his fishiness. Hanna imagined him fleeing sinuously, migrating as fish migrate, growing always more arrowy and lickery and fast. And now he had fled with Mrs Carr.

*

'Where's Mummy?' Jeremy asked at next day's lunch.

Mr Carr said nothing so Hanna felt it was up to her. 'Gone,' she said unimaginatively, 'to visit someone sick.'

'Who? Who's sick?' The children jinked their spoons.

'An aunt.'

'She hasn't got a sick aunt. She hasn't got an aunt at all.'

Mr Carr sniggered and was possibly less than sober.

'Little boys,' Hanna told Jeremy, 'don't always know everything that's going on.'

'Nor big ones either.' Mr Carr gave a shaky laugh and spilled his wine.

It was about eight p.m. a week later. Mr Carr stalked into the nursery.

'Are you all right? Everything OK?' It was an unfocused query.

'Yes.' Jeremy passed up the chance to complain.

Jane seized it: 'I miss my Mummy and I don't like Hanna. She smells.'

'We all smell,' her father told her, 'one way or another. Hanna's smells are the very seal and sign of decorous spinsterhood. Your mother's, on the other hand,' he spoke with venom, 'are anything but that. *They* . . .' He drew a menacing breath.

'Mr Carr,' warned Hanna, 'that will do.'

He stared at her. 'Yes,' he agreed, 'I suppose it will.' He threw back a limp lock with a coquettish movement. His face was sweating. 'Can you leave them,' he nodded at the children, 'and look after me?'

'Yes,' she told him. 'It's time for lights out, anyway.'

On the stairs down, Mr Carr lurched into her. 'I like your smell,' he confided. 'Womanly. Let me see, do I know what it is? Wool? Some sweat, that healthy soap, whatsitsname? Lifebuoy?'

'Pears.'

He shouted: 'That's it.' Then: 'Shall we go to your room?'

'The children . . .'

'Mmm. Let's go to Violet's then. We can violate her memory. Ha.'

'You're drunk.'

'I am. Do you mind?'

'No.'

When they reached Mrs Carr's room, Mr Carr quickly took off his clothes. He draped his trousers carefully over a chair and Hanna had the impression that he might be forgetting that it was not his wife with whom he was getting ready to go to bed. She made to slip out of the room but he caught her arm as she passed.

'No bloody bathing and bideting,' he said. 'Honest smells, Hanna.'

When she got back to the bedroom he was in bed.

'Come in.' He made some minimal move.

Hanna got in. She put a tentative hand on his shoulder but felt uncomfortable doing this. Mr Carr's shoulder was covered with sparse hairs which felt to the touch like sand on a picnic plate. She lay stiffly beside him. Minutes passed. Then a finger applied pressure to one of her nipples.

'Great nannyish boobs,' said Mr Carr. 'Take me in your arms, Hanna.' He gave something like a whimper, then whispered: 'Mother me.'

Hanna tried to get a hand under his back but he lay inert and didn't accommodate it. 'I'm afraid,' she said, 'I've never done this before.'

'Done what?'

'Anything.'

'Shit,' said Mr Carr. Then: 'You mean you're a virgin?'

'Yes.'

After an extended silence, Mr Carr rose and began to stumble about. He seemed suddenly drunker and the room full of obstacles. 'G-g-g . . .' he gnashed, 'odd.' And gathered his trousers off their chair which promptly fell. 'Sorry,' he said in its direction, fumbling on the floor, though he might have been talking to her. 'Inadequate,' he exclaimed angrily, abandoning the effort to set it on its legs. 'Utterly . . .' He made some grunts of exasperation. 'I . . . you know . . . hell.' Thrusting, at a breast-stroke, through apparently buoyant air, he made it to the door which clicked behind him. Hanna was left more alone than ever in Mrs Carr's baroque, satiny, sea-green cave of a room. After the creaking, then silent stairs had revealed him to be truly gone, she collected her clothes and left.

*

She went on running his house and he, to her relief, did not attempt apologies or talk to her at all. Apart from the children, neither did anyone else. Hanna had not learned Italian and there was no point in starting now for Mr Carr had decided to leave.

'Mad to have come here,' he said. 'A bloody disaster.'

It was November. Mercury-bright water dripped from ilexes, swelled in cypress globes, seeped through the roof.

'We'll take a flat in Paris,' Mr Carr promised his children. 'For Christmas. Mummy likes Paris.'

Hanna filled the large bath-tub with water and scented this with oils left behind by Mrs Carr. Lying in it, she considered the body which she had for twenty-nine years kept alive, well, unused and apparently insufficiently clean. Every month she had stanched its flow of superfluous blood. Was anything the matter with it?

The men in Poggibonsi thought there was. So, it seemed, did Mr Carr.

Brutta?

But if good looks were so important, why had Mrs Carr gone off with the ugly Elio? Clearly ugly was as ugly did. She considered how Elio had done. At table – safe in her social inequality – she watched him. 'I . . .' he kept saying. 'I . . . I . . .' It was every third word out of his mouth and, when you weren't attending, the sounds rushed together to make the *aiaiai* of a wailing Latin. But sharp. Enough to cut himself. Once or twice when Hanna was thinking no good of him, he had caught her eye, shaking clasped hands comically as though to ask forgiveness – then gone back to courting Mrs Carr.

'You *are* a fool, Elio,' Mrs Carr was too suddenly assaulted to make any but the most general protest.

Hanna, with hindsight, felt she had known all along what was happening, even feared for him. He was like a mobile, one of those gleaming chrome toys – a spring or coil – which when touched gives off high, haunting sounds, whirls, captivates and is so shoddily frail that one is afraid it may be knocked over. Elio was rash.

'One must break rules,' he had declared one evening. 'It reinforces them, reminds people what they're for. Otherwise they forget. Take the one about violating hospitality. I'll bet it never crosses your mind,' he leaned his face into Mr Carr's, 'that someone you've invited to your house might try to take advantage? Diddle you in some way? Hnn?' He laughed.

Mr Carr had backed away. Hanna was amused.

'I,' Elio told them, 'am a gipsy. Oh not by choice, but I lost a country and so I am. I look in on your solid households and envy your protective taboos. Perhaps I understand them better than you do?'

As no one took this up, he lightened his tone. 'I really am a gipsy,' he claimed. 'I play the Flamenco guitar.'

Some evenings later he turned up with one and played it very badly.

'God, the nerve,' Mr Carr was astounded. 'Has he no sense of the ridiculous?'

'You're the children's nanny then?' Elio stared at Hanna, classifying her in his mind. 'You come from the world of nurseries where fingernails grow into knives.' He picked up Hanna's manicured hand. 'Struwwelpeter,' he footnoted. His glance was carnivorous but he swivelled it back at once to Mrs Carr. He had, however, seen Hanna if only for a moment. His look had been sharp as a pin. She recalled and enjoyed it until she had worn the memory to a blur. It was rarely, almost never, that she felt someone had *seen*—perhaps liked?—her, Hanna, the woman behind the nanny, behind the name, herself.

'Me,' she whispered now, lying in her bath and remembering Elio's stare. 'Me.' But she couldn't focus on herself and the more she tried the more unjelled and colourless that self became until it seemed to dissolve and float off on the scented steam of Mrs Carr's bath oil. Like a crab unshelled, she felt herself adrift. If a friend had said 'You're tough, Hanna', she would have been. If they'd said 'You're vulnerable', she might have been that. But there was no one to say anything.

Under the drunken impulsions of her eye, the bathroom shifted. She and Mr Carr had taken to drinking too much Chianti over their monosyllabic meals. She turned on the hot tap, letting it flow until her blood seethed and the water tightened on her flesh like hands.

December was wet. Evergreens bulged like steamed artichokes. Lawns frilled with mud. Hanna and the children spent hours building cities with Lego. In her spare time Hanna read.

'Our last nanny was always writing letters. She got loads too. How come you don't? Haven't you any friends?'

'Some. But we don't write.'

'Mummy and Daddy don't either. They telephone. The telephone,' Jeremy added as an afterthought, 'makes Daddy cry.'

Hanna had been insulted again in Poggibonsi and now avoided the place. Once or twice she drove Jane and Jeremy to tea-parties in Florence or took them to the Cascine zoo to see the camel. He was a North-African like Elio, a mangy, melancholy beast who finally bit Jeremy. The little boy wept and Hanna kissed his swollen, mussel-shell blue hand to make it well.

'I love Hanna,' Jeremy said afterwards.

'I do too,' Jane said competitively.

Hanna went through the changes she might have with a lover: affection, distrust, jealousy of the absent Mrs Carr whom of course they really loved and who kept up a telephone flirtation with her absent family.

Jane was being bathed. Her freckled limbs, plunging about in the foam, were like flurries of oatmeal.

'Did you have bubble baths when you were small?'

'No.' Hanna remembered austerities. 'You're spoilt,' she said with an affectionate lunge at this slick package of pampered flesh. Jane evaded her. 'I've got soap in my eyes,' she wept.

'That'll be better before you're twice married.'

'Will I be? Were you? Even once?'

'No.'

'Is it too late for you now? How old are you?'

'Old.' Hanna made an aged face. 'Ancient.' She pulled her eyes slittily to the sides.

'Yes,' the child assessed soberly. 'Much older than my Mummy.'

'No. Actually,' Hanna unslitted her eyes, 'I think I'm younger.'

'You're years and *years* older,' sang Jane swimming back and forth on her hands, face down, feet kicking. 'A man in the park the other day asked *were* you my Mummy. Because you're English too, you know. But I said "no", you couldn't be my Mummy, could you?'

'Well . . .'

'I don't look like you,' Jane said with satisfaction. 'I look like her. I have her eyes and her hair and when I grow bigger I'll have breasts like her and hair here and . . .'

'Yes,' said Hanna repressively.

'And Jeremy will be like Daddy and have a winkle this big.'

Jane's hands sketched an enormous, impossible penis.

'That's enough now. Wash.'

But Jane, seeing that she had managed to touch off exasperation, determined to fan it. She grasped the loofah and held it in front of herself.

'Do you know what winkles are for, Hanna? I bet you haven't seen Daddy's?'

Hanna seized the loofah. Jane grabbed it back and in the struggle the small soapy body slid under water. Jane's face was covered. She spluttered, wriggled, rose and fell again. Then her reaching hand caught Hanna in the eye. Hanna, blinded, fumbled and felt herself push the child under. Jane's nails scratched Hanna's cheek and for moments Hanna could not tell whether her own fiercely reacting limbs were trying to save or drown the maddening, gulping little girl. Jane's feet threshed. Her frantic face went under again. Another moment and – Hanna had her out.

'You . . . pushed me,' accused the choking child. 'Under – you . . .'

'I didn't mean to,' Hanna told. 'It was a mistake. You had your finger in my eye. I couldn't see what I was doing.' She was shouting but it was at herself, for Jane, more intent on weeping than accusing, was not interested. Sobbing and panting, the child began to exploit and distance her adventure.

'I might have drowned. I nearly did drown.' It had become a boast.

'Yes,' Hanna admitted. 'You nearly did. Come on now. You'd better get out. Step onto this.'

Later, half in dream and half awake, Hanna replayed the scene with variations which chilled and bewildered her. Only one thing emerged from a turmoil of shame and nervous exhaustion: she had had an impulse – brief, brief but there – to drown the little girl.

The following week Mr Carr went away. A few days later he telephoned and gave Hanna instructions to close up the villa, leave the keys with the estate agent, pack the children's things and fly with them to Paris. He and Mrs Carr would meet them at Orly airport.

'Violet says to make sure the children are warmly dressed.'

He sounded, Hanna thought, like a child who has got over-excited at a party and hopes not to show this lest he be taken away. So what had happened to Elio then? Ousted? Or was Mr Carr putting up with him? No, she decided. He was too perky for that. Ousted. Definitely. She wondered how Elio was taking that.

All the way to Pisa and Paris she used dead moments to wonder. Ousted, Elio fitted more easily into her own fantasies. Defeat domesticated him. Poor Elio, she thought, poor greedy blackbird chased from the strawberry patch. She laughed.

After Customs, the children rushed, limbs wild, into the octopodal embrace of their two parents. Hanna waited with a small, contingent smile.

'So what do you hope for?'

Hanna shrugged. 'Nothing really,' she said. 'I suppose.'

Elio sighed. 'Your mother was a ghoul all right. Ate your flesh, anaesthetized you with dream, kept you with her, doing time until she died. You're lucky she ever did.'

Hanna was hurt, sorry she'd confided. 'Don't you fantasize?' she challenged.

He drooped, but comically, guying it. 'It's my vice.' Some of the starch had gone out of him though he had shot from his shop like a cuckoo from its clock when she walked past: 'Hanna! Miss McKenna!'

She had jumped with surprise, then remembered that she had known all along he had a shop here, rue de Seine.

'You're the nanny,' he said. 'I recognized you at once.'

For a moment she wondered was he hoping for a message from Mrs Carr. If he was he hid his hopes.

'I saw you look in the window,' he said. 'Did you know this was my shop? Come inside.' He closed the door. 'You're cold. You never know how cold you are until you reach the warmth. Have you time for a grog?'

She had.

'We'll go to a café then. Wait.'

He locked the door behind them, leaving a card which promised a quick return. In the café the old Elio reappeared. Talk revived him and he began to brag. Remembering that Hanna must know of at least one of his defeats, he mocked himself. 'Fantasy,' he admitted, 'dangerous damn stuff.'

'Oh I,' she told him, 'couldn't survive without it.'

He drew her out. She talked of her mother but the picture of the two women lone and dreaming in their empty house depressed him.

'*Merde!*' he groaned. 'The lives people lead. I know it. I know it. Especially in the provinces. Devouring each other. Your mother was a ghoul.' He was soberer than she remembered. 'Yes,' he admitted when she remarked on this. 'I get low. I function best in company. That's common enough, you know.'

He was looking right at her which sent her voice kiting up.

'Know?' she cried. 'I know nothing.' It sounded like a bid for sympathy but she was sorry when she got it. She didn't want his pity and pity, it seemed, might have to be their currency.

Later, as it was raining, he drove her back to the Carrs' but let her off at the corner of their street. She saw he didn't want to meet them.

'Come by again,' he invited.

She did. He gave her advice about what to see in Paris. Another day he took her to see some paintings. A *vernissage*. There was nothing intimate about their chats but Hanna imagined intimacies with Elio. She had overheard a scene, almost certainly the final one, between him and Mrs Carr.

A few days after her arrival in Paris she had been in her room in the Carrs' flat, standing by the window, when she heard them talking on the balcony next to her own. Mrs Carr had a clear, carrying voice.

'What difference do reasons make,' she was saying. 'Let's say I'm bored.'

Elio said something inaudible. Then Hanna heard 'obsessive' and 'intensity' . . .

Mrs Carr interrupted: 'I think you're a bit deranged.'

'I told you,' Elio's voice was not quite clear. He was leaning over the balcony, 'I had only my folly to offer.'

'A fine phrase.'

'You dislike the reality?'

'Sex-talk? My husband's better at the practice.'

'God, you are a bitch.'

'Do you think so?'

'You think sex is a branch of gym.'

'I like a *little* action.'

'You probably think it's good for your health. It isn't, you know, it's a demonic force which you unleash at your . . .'

'Peril.' Mrs Carr supplied. 'Yes-ss.' she sighed. 'I do recall.'

'So you won't reconsider . . .'

'I won't.'

'Goodbye then, Violet.' Abruptly there was a sound of sobbing. Elio's voice gulped, 'Take no notice, I . . .' The two left the balcony. Minutes later Hanna heard the flat door close and Mrs Carr walk back to her room.

'Demonic,' she thought afterwards. 'Unhealthy. At your peril.' The words excited her. She dreamed of Elio. In her dream she slid towards him along damp pavements. '*Brutto,*' she whispered, '*brutto.*' The word reverberated. It meant a lot of things which she held in her apprehension, distantly, as one might the string of a kite.

'I overheard you,' she thought of saying to him, 'talking to Mrs Carr. I was in the next room and I heard.' She imagined herself staring at him with a stare hard with a reflection of Mrs Carr's cruelty. It would precipitate the intimacy he was denying her.

This dreaming was in contrast to the sedate meetings she actually had with Elio. They had become a habit. After shopping, she would call in and he would brew tea on a ring he kept in the back of the shop. Business seemed slow or perhaps that was how the antique trade was. There were rarely any customers to interrupt. Hanna found Elio's wares depressing: snuffy, reeking of dead lives. 'Antique' to her was just a word for 'old'. She knew it gave the wormy stuff value but it was a value which escaped her as so many seemed to do: religion which she had relinquished after some distrustful flirting with it in school, beauty – well not much hope for her there. She tried not to think of love. When Elio mentioned politics, she burst out with: 'Isn't that just another surrogate to take our minds off our own emptiness? Do happy people ever care for politics?'

Elio stared.

'I'm sorry,' she said. 'I don't know what's the matter with me. Maybe I should go home.'

'Home to Ireland or home to the Carrs?'

'I don't know. Both perhaps.'

'Come home with me,' he suggested, adding, 'It's closing time anyway.'

They paused at a supermarket. 'I'm not much of a cook,' Elio warned but knew just what to buy, filling his basket with deft speed.

Outside his flat he stopped. 'I don't usually bring people here. Except . . . well. Don't be embarrassed.' Obviously embarrassed himself, he opened the door. Hanna groped after him for he had, in his sudden doubts as to the taste of his interior decoration, put on no lights. Plunging at a cupboard illuminated from within like a tabernacle – it *was* a tabernacle, perhaps one of those he had scrounged from Tuscan priests – now doing duty as a bar, he offered 'Whisky? Gin? My body and blood?'

Hanna fell over something soft. 'For Christ's sake, Elio,' she moaned from the floor. 'Is there no proper light? Put something *on*.'

He did and she found herself supine among a scatter of floor cushions. She looked about her. 'Jesus.' She began to laugh.

The place was upholstered in purples and reds, their deep-piled softness pierced here and there by the glint of miniature Pakistani mirrors. It was furnished with pieces of Gothic-Revival Gothic and what must be Moorish stuff Elio had brought back from North Africa. No chairs. All lights were indirect and arranged to spotlight phallic statuary, paintings, blown-up cartoons.

'Do you hate it?'

She felt she must absolve him. 'No,' she assured. 'It's like a child's tree-house. I suppose I think of children because everything's so low. It's all for fun, isn't it? Nothing's functional. How do you eat here?'

'I eat in the kitchen. Or out. I don't invite people much, except . . .'

Except, she thought, people like Mrs Carr.

Later he said, 'I wouldn't want you to feel . . .'

'Insulted at being brought here?' Men – she recalled from some advice-column – only worried about appearing to lack respect for women who did not attract them. 'Don't worry about my suscep-tibilities,' she said bitterly. 'I'm a magnet for respect. An iron virgin and near-nun. I'll probably stay chaste until I die. I don't doubt my straits are as impassable as the mine-strewn Suez Canal.'

This seemed to arouse Elio. Or it may have been something else. Perhaps the sheer mechanics of his cushioned, chairless flat had caught him in his own seducer's trap, for he was obliged to recline beside her and, moments later, relinquishing his whisky, was rolling with her among conducive billows. Hanna grappled him to her with inexpert greed. All angles and elbows, she might have been eating him, fancied that she *was* biting bloody, pulpy, fruit-size snatches of his flesh which turned from poison-green to red to purple in the reflections of a rotating light beamed beyond them at a bronze lion who was doing something to a nymph.

'Easy does it. Are you really a virgin?' he marvelled.

'Yes.' She remembered practicalities. 'Should I be doing something in the bathroom?'

'Don't worry,' he soothed. 'I'm not very potent.' But he was.

'My God!' Surprised himself: 'I've never been like this. You're a witch.'

'Will it be all right then?'

'Don't worry.'

She groaned.

'You're bleeding.'

'I told you.'

'Does it hurt?'

'Yes.'

Elio was ecstatic. 'Blood.' He showed it to her on his fingers. 'Once the creature has reproduced itself, it becomes superfluous. Sex points to death. Blood is the sign.' He wagged red fingers, mumbling on with what she thought of as his gothicries.

'Oh Elio.' She might have been drunk, dreaming, dead.

'Here, I'll get you a towel. Lucky they're red. First time that's come in useful. The carpets too . . .' He mopped, muttered.

'Am I your first virgin then?'

He admitted this and his excitement. 'Usually,' he confessed, 'I can't manage at all. Too cerebral. I've been to more shrinks . . . never mind that now. It's over. I can tell. Thanks to you. Another drink?'

He brought in the bottle, holding it phallicly to his belly. He *had* a belly, she noted, and a poor physique generally – to judge by statues and Mr Carr. Not that she cared, or only to fear that being without beauty himself, he might need it in a woman.

'Elio,' she began to ask, then didn't for fear of drawing attention to her lacks.

He had taken off again on his exultant crowing. 'Let me taste your virgin's blood. Ha,' he almost sang. 'Another taboo violated. I wonder has it magic properties?'

It hadn't.

Next time, hindered by embarrassment before a scene perhaps mentally over-rehearsed by both, they were over-eager, awkward and failed to connect. Elio, to both their humiliation, was unable to make love.

'Please, please don't worry,' Hanna implored. She was stricken. 'It doesn't,' she heard herself produce an imitation of Mrs Carr at her most hostessy, 'matter the teeniest bit. Truly,' she went on. Her voice flew upwards; out of control, it rang tinnier by the minute as she strove to get off the track on which she was being borne as helplessly as once when she was eleven and her roller-skate had got caught in a down-hill tram-line. 'Or if it does matter,' she flailed, 'let's not stay here in the flat. I mean let's not if you'd rather not because it's all the same to me – or rather it's not but – oh Elio,' she interrupted herself. 'Do tell me to shut up.'

An awful joke had occurred to her: was she a reverse Gorgon whose horrid head softened instead of turning men to stone? It was not a joke to share.

The sorrow of it was that she had been made so happy the last time by his triumph. They had held hands afterwards and this gesture had undone Hanna's defences. She had confided the depths of her need. A mistake? Loneliness did frighten people off, she knew. She tried to cast it far into the past. It had been *before*, long ago, she emphasized.

'Now I can remember us here together and that will scout loneliness.'

Maybe Elio couldn't stand such responsibility? Or was it her looks? While he had been making love to her, she had fancied herself attractive – wasn't she, after all, attracting *him*? Now she needed desperately to coquet, ask 'Am I ugly?', be reassured. She didn't dare. Their vanities were too vulnerably entangled. But the fault *must* be his. It had to be. The blue jokes and red flat proved it. They were palliatives to some secret hindrance, stimuli to arouse a weak or impacted libido. But what then could she have done? She had done all she knew how. Game for anything, and for any role he might assign, she had come to their second rendezvous scrubbed clean as a deck, scented like a cosmetic shop, burning and deliquescent, ready and randy. Then Elio had had a débâcle, a fiasco . . . She was soon familiar with all the sad names for the non-event.

He loaded her with books and she staggered up the Carrs' stairway, looking like someone planning to take a Ph.D. in *érotologie*. Heavy in her arms were Bataille's *œuvre*, Klossowski's ditto, *Emmanuelle*, *O*, half the publishing list of J. J. Pauvert. Elio had confided a fear of becoming utterly impotent. She, he had been sure, was to be his saviour, his virgin patron. He wasn't yet convinced that she couldn't manage this but felt it would be trickier than at first foreseen. She must acquire a little science. Sex-in-the-head preceded sex-in-the-bed. Please, please, for both their sakes, would Hanna devote a little sympathetic interest to his problem, read . . .

The stuff horrified her. It was mostly in stilted French so locked to her anyway, but there was enough in English to upset her.

'Elio,' she begged shyly. 'instead of all this, couldn't we try to maybe *like* each other. Isn't that . . . I mean . . .' The naivety of her plea shamed her even as she tried to put the rags of it together. Wasn't it like offering a home remedy to someone afflicted with a dread disease? But the question mattered too much to be suppressed. 'Doesn't liking the other person,' she begged, 'come into this at all?'

She gave back the books.

'I can't read them,' she said. 'My French isn't up to it. I never went to college, you know. I was nursing my mother . . .'

'That ghoul.'

'Then in the convent we learned a very different sort of French. Prayers. Idioms . . .'

Mention of the convent revived Elio. 'Do you feel sinful?' he hoped. 'When you went home that first time, did you?'

'No.'

This seemed to cast him down. '*Merde!*' he railed, pleased at the chance to take off on a bit of rhetoric. '*Merde!* The harm Freud has done. Not to mention Hippocrates.' He was enjoying himself. 'All those men of science,' he camped, 'with their Epsom-salts mentality. And there *you* are shedding your sense of awe as fast as your knickers. They take the shadow out of life and without the shadow,' Elio clutched his genitals, 'there is no substance.' He stood up from the bed – they had been lying on it inconclusively. 'I have a surprise. It is to remind you of the dark dimension. The taboo . . . We . . .' Elio's head was lost in a wardrobe made of dark wood. It was, Hanna remembered him telling her, one of the ones he had bought in Italy and had once belonged in a sacristy. 'Shut your eyes,' he directed from inside it in a clothy voice. Hanna did. There was a rustling, a smell of mothballs, woodworm, second-hand clothes, then: 'Now,' he commanded. 'Look.'

Hanna looked. Elio stood before her dressed as a priest about to say mass. A touch stiffly, he began to rotate so as to let her have the full benefit of his get-up. Wherever he'd got it, it was genuine: purple vestments as though for Lent or mourning, white alb and, flung incongruously over one shoulder like a football fan's team-colours, a stole.

'Well,' he asked solemnly, 'do I remind you of lost innocence, violated First Communion vows?' His hands searched for a liturgical gesture, lost it, waved. Flapping like a beaten rug, he leaped and landed on the bed.

Hanna guffawed. It was involuntary at first: a nervous suck-in of air like a fist hitting her teeth, for he had in fact taken away her breath. Then, as she became aware of what he had done, she kept it up. Nanny's lore came to her aid; laughing them out of it was the best policy with outrageous children. 'Goodness, Elio,' she wheezed, 'you do look a guy.' I, she thought angrily, am not the one in need of stimulus. And besides: 'Elio, aren't you Jewish? If you need to violate taboos, surely they should be your own? Why don't you dress as a Rabbi? Produce your prayer-shawl, isn't that what you call it? Your phylacteries?' Mocking him. Laughing. Scandalized.

He had begun to droop, his bottle shoulders sank to nothing and the gilt-stiff, fiddle-back chasuble hung on them like a rag on a stick.

'Well, has it worked?'

White, furious, he yanked the chasuble over his head, dragged off the rest of the gear and flung it in the wardrobe.

'Shut up!' he roared.

'I'm only trying to help.'

'Stoppit.'

She left. They met again. Apparently he was as uneager as she to give up, but they did not go back for a while to his flat. Having had a fight, they were now more intimate and forgiving. She fancied he saw them as co-workers on a project. But it was a tricky business, volatile.

'Women,' he pontificated, 'like to feel righteous and noble. That crushes a man. Even Violet who, God knows, was committing adultery in her husband's house, wanted to feel righteous about it. So she had to pretend that there was affection involved, a relationship. That's the word *you're* groping after, by the way: relationship. I'll save you the groping since you're new to the game. It's the word you want all right. All *I* want is a fuck.'

Hanna said nothing; he laughed. 'Passing up your cue, eh? Being magnanimous? You're supposed to ask why I can't deliver even that. God, this is a fascinating dialogue. Me playing both parts.'

When things went well – after a good meal of couscous in the rue de la Huchette, for instance, eaten with a lot of relaxing strong Algerian wine, she could risk touching him. But it was like approaching a dog who has been beaten too often. Her intention had to be made clear in advance.

'Just your hand, Elio. A gesture of peace.'

'Afraid I'll be afraid you're trying to arouse . . . ?'

For any caress could be taken as a challenge.

'Are we both horrible people?' she wondered.

'A marriage made in heaven? Like calling to like?'

'No, I was working round to an apology. For laughing at you,' she risked, 'that time you dressed up as a priest. You understand I felt offended. I felt you were trying to put me at a distance. Your gothicries do that anyway. All that stagey stuff you keep around. As if you were afraid of being taken seriously. Tied down. *Is* that what it is? A defence?'

'Against what? Love? Marriage? Being possessed by another woman?'

'Who possessed you before?'

'My bloody mother. A ghoul like yours only she didn't really gain possession of me the way she would have liked. The war saved me and she died alone, penniless, in great squalor which would be the part she hated most. Not that I had much choice. My father, very sensibly, tried to take both of us with him into hiding. We were Jews. It was the war. But would she come? Not on your – her, ha, life. You see it would have meant joining the household of my father's legitimate wife. Playing second fiddle. So she stayed and died of pride. And resentment.'

'Against you?'

'Me. My father. Time. The world. She resented everything. A righteous, beautiful, smug, possessive fool of a woman. A woman.'

'Mmm.'

Later he said: 'You are a kind person. You don't seize your chances to bitch. Or only some of them. That's good. Rare. Actually,' he went on, 'we're in danger of getting too friendly. Friendship doesn't go with sex. I think of you as a decent sort, *une copine*. Maybe we should leave it at that?'

The next time they met, he said he'd had a dream about his mother. 'She was dressed to kill. Pun intended. In tight silk. And we were in a children's park somewhere in Oran. She was sliding down a slide. At first it looked quite ordinary, but when she reached the bottom I saw that it was set with vertical razor-blades and slices of bloody flesh and silk had been rashered off my mother's thighs. Like long streamers. Then I woke up. That's the sort of dream I have about her. Guilt dreams. She haunts me. A ghoul, you see. A vampire.'

Hanna whirled the Kir in her glass. As usual they were in a bar. The red liquid lapped the sides.

'Dreams,' she said, 'are usually made up. Or stolen from psychological literature.'

'You mean I'm lying?'

'Or looking for some absolution. I don't know. A chance maybe to blame present inadequacies on past ones. You're playing games anyway. Keeping me and probably everyone else at a distance. I'm not bitching, but there's no point meeting at all if I can't say this. I'm fond of you. I don't ask you to say you are of me. You tolerate my presence. But you invent game after game to retreat into. What's the use of pretending we're even friends?'

'A woman,' said Elio, 'who throws a man's sexual failure in his face is abusing confidence. To say the least.'

'Who said "sexual"?'

'Who was thinking of anything else? Now or ever?'

She lost her temper. 'You parade your weakness,' she accused. 'It's a wonder you don't apply for a card saying "sexual cripple". It might get you preferential treatment on the Paris buses.'

He said *she* was an emotional cripple, a parasite, clinging, boring, begging, ugly. They did not meet for weeks.

They did not telephone either. She missed him, feeling her loneliness incalculably more than she had before. She supposed this meant she was, in one of the contradictory ways which fester beneath that umbrella phrase, 'in love with him'. God help her then. He was, after all, a silly man who used his considerable ingenuity to torment himself and everyone who came within his orbit. But then what did she know of men? Or love? Or, she remembered his wry dismissive word, 'relationships'? See-sawing between desire and rage, she stayed awake nights thinking of him and quarrelled as soon as she had summoned a credible image with which to quarrel. Imagining his flesh next to her own, she dealt it kisses which had a tendency to turn cannibalic. 'God,' she thought, catching herself, 'I'm the ghoul. He should watch it with me. I'm the sort of woman who kills from jealousy. I must tell him next time we meet. It might excite him. A new game. I owe him a game.'

But she knew she was playing one with herself: deceiving herself into thinking she was not alone or that there was a likelihood of there being a second chance, another meeting. Whereas, at the end of two weeks, it became clear that there was not. Even as friends, as decent sorts, risking a brief relaxing of defences in each others' company over cheapish drinks in small cafés. *She* could not take the initiative. She waited though, moping, on her free days, through a freezing, greasy Paris. Shoppers and drinkers were all clearly plugged into social circuits. They moved about in groups or couples. Not she. She knew the routines of loneliness: the brisk walk which suggests purpose when there is none, the art of pumping trivial errands up into quests. She spent a free Wednesday choosing a birthday present for Jeremy although she knew it would be one of the least regarded of his gifts. When Mrs Carr told her she could have an extra day off as *she* would be taking the children to the circus, the leisure loomed like a void. Unable to bear it, she rode a bus across river to the Left Bank, walked up the rue de Seine and paused at Elio's shop window. He was with a customer and didn't see her. She walked around a draughty block and came back. The customer was still there. She walked to the Rhumerie and forced herself to drink two grogs. When she returned the card saying 'the proprietor will be back in ten minutes' hung unconvincingly in the window. Fifteen minutes later he *was* back but the customer was still with him. Hanna walked in. The bell jangled. Elio turned.

His body, shy, hunched, bulging in the wrong places, reminded her of birds who fluff against the cold and so look fattest when hungriest in the lean winter. They were two of a kind, but perhaps that was what he couldn't bear? She felt herself cringe inside her clothes.

'Hanna.' He left the customer. 'I'm so glad,' he whispered. 'I've been waiting for your call. Every day.'

'*You've* been waiting?' She was astounded. 'Why didn't *you* call *me*?'

'How could I? After what . . . had been said?'

He avoided her eye which gave her a chance to stare at him. He looked – was the word 'haggard'? He gripped her arm above the elbow. Tightly. Painfully. More like a policeman than a lover. He's as clumsy, she thought, as I. Neither of us knows this game at all. 'I'm busy now,' he whispered. 'A big sale.' He nodded at the customer. 'A collector. Look. Here are the keys of the flat. Go there

35

in a taxi and wait. I'll be along as soon as the deal's clinched. I'll phone if there's a delay. OK?'

The taxi followed the route Elio had taken on their first evening and Hanna, sitting in it, experienced one of those abrupt and total reversals which must, she supposed, be peculiar to lovers, though perhaps people who dealt with danger knew them too. Her humours turned turtle. Her blood sang; her body chemistry had changed; her mind was at work on new data: he had been afraid to ring, needed her, was shy, was inexpert, *needed* her. It was up to her to take over the – defiantly she mouthed the word – relationship. Up to her. Power rose in her and she gave the taximan a celebrative tip.

In the flat she made herself a drink and poked fearlessly about. It was the first time she had been here alone. Brothelly refuge. She put on all the lights, puzzled out the cleverer porny paintings, had another drink and went into the bedroom. Here, framed in Art Nouveau tortoiseshell, was Elio's mother. She gazed at Hanna through reproachful, ultra-feminine eyes deepened by that smudgy shadow one always seemed to get in pre-war photographs. As though she were wearing kohl which, come to think of it, living in North Africa, she probably was.

'Hi, sister,' Hanna tilted her glass at the photo. '*Salut, hypocrite, ma semblable, ma sœur.*'

The mother in the photo was about Hanna's own age.

'*Ma semblable,*' Hanna repeated with tipsy humour and walked to the wardrobe where she seemed to remember seeing – yes, where there was a whole section filled with women's clothes. Hanna stroked the hanging garments. There were furs here, beaded dresses, suedes and silks, fringy and embroidered things drooping from padded hangers with that nineteen-thirtiesish slouch which manages, before the dress is put on at all, to suggest languor, femininity and a sloppy contempt.

'The ghoul's.' Hanna sniffed a stretch of scented cloth.

She knew the style from old things of Mummy's which she had been allowed to use as a child, dressing up in them to play at weddings on wet or lonely afternoons. But none of Mummy's stuff had been as fancy as this. Oran clearly had been far more fashionable than Dublin. At any rate showier.

'Think of his saving them,' she marvelled. 'Bringing them here from Algeria. And then sleeping in the room with them. For years.'

Again she ran a hand down the rich surface of a dress and, almost before quite knowing what she was doing, had taken off her own and slipped this one on. It fitted more or less well and Hanna looked for a mirror to arrange it better. The bathroom had only a shaving mirror but she did manage with its help to fasten the zipper and smooth the silky creation down over her hips. It was dark sea-green, cut on the bias and made of a sort of shimmering material with a watermark. Returning to the wardrobe, Hanna found a fur which she snuggled around her neck and a cloche hat which she pulled firmly on, stuffing her hair up under it to give herself a period look. Next she found some gloves and shoes covered with finely pleated crêpe de Chine. The feel of the expensive stuffs was euphoric and Hanna could not help hoping that they might improve her appearance. Fine feathers after all made fine birds. Did they not?

'Am I still ugly?' she wondered. 'Was I ever *ugly*?'

Elio had said she was once, but he had been in a rage. The men of Poggibonsi had said it calmly but they could well have been anti-English or even using the word '*brutta*' as a secretly erotic caress. Maybe, Hanna dared to wonder, she might even be beautiful? She began to caress herself through clingy, sensuous stuff.

'Hanna,' she whispered, 'Hanna.'

Elio's mother gazed from her photograph and Hanna felt some of the other woman's feminine, flirtatious softness melt her own limbs.

'I want to *see* myself,' she murmured. But the shaving mirror was too small. Then she remembered the ceiling mirror which hung, huge and pale as a sky, over the bed.

Carefully she climbed onto this, lay on her back, smoothed down the skirt and sleeves of the clingy gown and looked upwards. Above her, all in green, gloved and hatted, lying with the incongruous composure of a corpse, floated a nineteen-thirties lady on a red eiderdown.

Beautiful? Ugly?

The lady caressed her own body from shoulders to hips and didn't seem to know.

When at last she unglued her glance, it was to find Elio standing – how long had he been there? – in the bedroom door.

'*Maman!*' he whispered, '*ma petite maman!*' And started to take off his clothes.

At the level from which Hanna was viewing his erection, it looked as big and vigorous as if his legs were straddling a broomstick. Then he was on top of her. 'Lovely witch,' he groaned, 'lovely, lovely . . . *Beautiful* Hanna!'

Daughters of Passion

There was a story about her in the *Mail*. A phrase jumped off the page: '. . . the twisted logic of the terrorist mind . . .' Journalists! She'd have spat if she'd had the spittle; but her mouth was dry. 'Violence,' someone had said, 'is the only way to gain a hearing for moderation.' That was reckoning without the press.

The argument broke open, porous as cheese. *Cheese* . . . She could smell the reek of it, pinching her nostrils.

Thoughts escaped her. This was the twelfth day of her hunger strike and energy was running low. Half a century ago, in Brixton Gaol, the Lord Mayor of Cork had died after a seventy-four-day fast. A record? Maybe. But how *much* of him could have survived those seventy-four days to die? A sane mind? The ability to choose? Surely not? Surely all that was left in the end would have been something like the twitch in a chicken-carcass, a set of reflexes primed like an abandoned robot's? Her own mind was bent on sabotaging her will. 'Eat,' her organism signalled slyly to itself in divers ways. It slurped and burped the message, registered it by itch, wind-pain, cold, hunger, sophistries. Sum ergo think. But thinking used up energy. Better just to dream: let images flicker the way they used to do years and years ago on the school cinema-screen. Then too it had been a case of energy running low. The generator went on the blink every time films were shown in the barn and that was often, for the hall was constantly being re-modelled. The nuns were great builders.

'Come,' they coerced visitors, 'come see our improvements.'

Change thrilled them. The stone might have been part of them-selves: a collective shell. Meanwhile, on film nights, rain drummed out the sound track and a draughty screen distorted the smile of

Jennifer Jones playing Bernadette. The barn was cold but discomfort was welcomed in the convent. Waiting for the centrally-heated hall put in time while waiting for heaven.

She missed the community feeling.

Her vision shifted. Bricks and mortar from the nuns' hall had turned to butcher's meat. She was choking. Her throat had dried, its sides seeming to clap together. She pictured it like an old boot, drying until the tongue inside it shrivelled. It itched. Food could drive any other consideration from her mind. Images decomposed and went edible, like those trick paintings in which whole landscapes turn out to be made up of fruit or sausages. She could smell sausages. Fat beaded on them. Charred skins burst and the stuffing pushed through slit bangers in a London pub. Three sausages and three half lagers, please. Harp or Heineken. Yes, draught. Could we have the sausages nice and crispy. Make that six. A dab of mustard. Jesus! Eat this in remembrance. Oh, and three rolls of French bread. Thanks. Christ-the-pelican slits his breast to feed the faithful. Dry stuff the communion wafer but question not the gift host in my mouth. Mustn't laugh. Hurts. Where's the water mug? Tea in this one. They'd left it on purpose. The screws were surely hoping she'd eat in a moment of inattention. It hadn't happened though. Relax. Water. What a relief. Made one pee and the effort of getting up was painful but if she didn't drink her throat grew sandpapery. You wanted to vomit and there was nothing to vomit. A body could bring up its guts – could it?

Sitting up made her dizzy. She felt a pain around her heart. Lie back. Her mind though was clear as well water. At least she was too weak to get across the cell to that tray without catching herself. They'd left it there with the food she'd refused this morning or maybe yesterday. Not that she felt fussy. Easier now though that her body was subdued beyond tricking her.

Conviction hardened. It had come with habit. Maggy was here through chance.

'I'm sure I don't know,' the head screw had said, 'where you think this is going to get you. It's up to you, of course, to make your own decision.'

Cool, bored. Managing to convey her sense of all this as childish theatrics and a waste of everyone's time. She knew the system and the system didn't change just because some little Irish terrorist wouldn't eat her dinner. She was fair though, abiding by the Home Secretary's guidelines. Nobody had kicked Maggy or put a bag over her head. This screw looked as though such things were outside her experience which perhaps they were. One lot of prison employees might be unaware of what the other lot were doing. A clever division of labour: those needing clear consciences for television interviews and the like could *have* clear consciences. The best myths had a dose of truth to them.

It might have been easier if they *had* knocked her about: given her more reason to resist.

Dizzy had said, 'The trouble with you, Maggy, is that you're an adapter. I suppose orphans are. They're survivors and survivors adapt.'

She meant that Maggy listened to the other side: a woeful error since it weakened resolve. Look at her now ready to believe in the decency of that screw. 'Sneering Brit,' Dizzy would decide right off. She never called the English anything but 'Brits'.

'Ah come on, Maggy. *Be* Irish for Pete's sake. What did the Brits ever do for you or yours? Listen, it's a class war. Don't you see?'

Dizzy was of Anglo-Irish Protestant stock and had gone native in a programmed way. Her vocabulary was revolutionary. Her upper-class voice had learned modulation at the Royal Academy of Dramatic Art. This made her enterprises sound feasible, as though they had already been realized, then turned back into fiction for celebrating in, say, the Hampstead Theatre Club or one of those fringe places on the Euston Road.

Rosheen's style was more demotic. She sang in pubs and in the shower of the flat which Maggy had shared with her and Dizzy.

> Another marthyr for auld Oireland
> Another murther for the Crown . . .

More exasperating than sheer noise was the spasm in Rosheen's voice. Maggy suspected she got more pleasure from these laments than she did from sex. The two had got connected in Rosheen's life. She had married an unemployed Derryman who took out his frustrations by beating her until Dizzy coerced her into walking out on him. Missing him, Rosheen flowed warm water down her soapy body every morning and belted out verses about tombs, gallowses and losses which would never be forgotten. Defeats, in her ballads, were greater than victory; girls walked endlessly on the sunny side of mountains with sad but pretty names and reflected on the uselessness of the return of spring. Maggy despised herself for the rage Rosheen aroused in her.

'Well, it's all due to history, isn't it?'

The three had watched the Northern Ireland Secretary on the box some weeks before Maggy's arrest. Talking of how a political solution would make the I R A irrelevant – *great* acumen, God bless him! – he had the mild smile of one obliged to shoulder responsibility and take the brickbats.

He got Rosheen's goat. 'He gets my goat,' she said. Maggy winced.

'He gets on my tits,' said Dizzy to show solidarity. But the effect was different since Dizzy could talk any way she felt inclined whereas poor Rosheen was stuck in one register.

Maggy, who had known Rosheen since they were six, had for her the irritable affection one has for relatives. Also envy. They had made their first communion side by side dressed in veils and identical bridal gowns and Rosheen had made the better communion. Maggy, watching through falsely closed lids, had been stunned to see ecstasy on Rosheen's rather puddingy face. She had been hoping for ecstasy herself and it was only when she saw it come to Rosheen that she gave up and admitted to herself that Jesus had rejected her. It was a close equivalent to being jilted at the altar and in some ways she had never got over it.

'Your First Holy Communion,' Mother Theresa had promised, 'will be the most thrilling event in your whole lives.'

'Really?'

'Oh,' the nun conceded, 'there will, I suppose, be other excitements.' It was clear that she could not conceive of them. She had been teaching communion classes for forty years. Photographs of groups dressed in white veils lined her classroom walls. 'Strength will flow into you,' she promised. 'I don't mean,' she smiled at Rosheen who had made this mistake earlier, 'the sort of strength Batman has.'

The others gave Rosheen a charitable look. They were practising charity and she was its best recipient. Charity was for those to whom you could not bring yourself to accord esteem or friendship and in those days it had been hard to produce these for Rosheen, whose eyes were pink and from whose nostrils snot worms were always apt to crawl. You had to look away so as to give her a chance to sniff them back up. Even then you could sometimes see her, with the corner of your eye, using the back of her hand.

And then Rosheen had made the best communion.

It was not utterly unaccountable. The nuns had mentioned that the last shall be first. Their behaviour, however, made this seem unlikely. They preferred girls who knew how to use handkerchiefs, scored for the team and generally did them credit.

Maggy recalled quite clearly how, having finally got the wafer down her throat – to bite would have been sacrilegious, so this was slow – and still feeling no ecstasy, she had opened her eyes. All heads were bowed. The priest was wiping the chalice. Could he have made some mistake, she wondered, left out some vital bit of the ceremony so that the miracle had failed to happen? Maybe he would realize and make an announcement: 'Dearly beloved, it is my duty to inform you that transubstantiation has failed to take place. Due to an error, you have all received mere bread and may regard the ceremony up to now as a trial run. Please return to the altar . . .' These words became so real to Maggy that she nudged Rosheen who was kneeling beside her. 'Get up,' she whispered bossily. 'We're to go back . . .' She was arrested by Rosheen's face. It was alight. Colour from a stained-glass window had been carried to it by a sunbeam and blazed madly from her eyes, her nostrils and the lolling tip of her tongue. Rosheen smiled, rotated and then bowed her head. She looked like a drunk or a painted saint: ecstatic then? Could she be pretending? Maggy considered giving her a pinch but instead bowed her own head and concentrated on managing not to cry.

She was crying now. Hunger made you weepy. She'd been warned. It made you cold too, although she was wearing several jerseys and two pairs of leotards.

Rosheen had never been so right again. Probably she should never have left the convent. Someone had told Maggy that she had wanted to enter but the nuns wouldn't have her. Then she'd married Sean. That marriage had certainly not been made in heaven: it was a case of the lame leading the halt.

'A pair of babes in the wood,' was the opinion of Sean's mother, Mairéad.

Mairéad had come to London some months ago to see Sean and dropped round to Dizzy's flat. Maggy had been the only one in.

'Tell Rosheen I don't hold it against her that she left him.' Mairéad was a chain-smoking flagpole of a woman, stuck about with polyester garments so crackling new that they must surely have been bought for this trip. 'Half the trouble in the world,' she drew on her cigarette then funnelled smoke from her nostrils with an energy which invited harnessing, 'comes,' she said, 'from people asking too much of themselves.' She coughed. 'And of each other. Not that it's Sean's fault either. I'm not saying that. It's his nerves,' she told Maggy. 'They're shot to bits. What would you expect? When that wee boy was growing up he seen things happen to his family that shouldn't happen to an animal.' She let Maggy make tea and, drinking it, talked in a practised way about misfortune. 'She's at work then, is she? Well give her my best. I'm half glad I missed her. I only wanted her to know there were no hard feelings. Will you tell her that from me? No hard feelings,' she enunciated carefully as though used to dealing with drunks or children or maybe men with shot nerves. 'I'd have no right to ask her to nurse a man in Sean's condition. I know that. He's not normal any more than the rest of us.' She had a high laugh which escaped like a hiccup: 'Heheh! He was never strong. A seven-month baby. I never had the right food. Then the year he was sixteen it was nothing but them bustin' in and calling us fucking Fenian gets and threatening to blow our heads off. Every night nearly. That was the summer of 1971. They wrecked the house; stole things; ripped up the carpet. Four times they raided us before Sean left to come here. He's highly strung and his nerves couldn't stand it. He still has nightmares. Ulcers. Rosheen could tell you. Sure it has to come out some way. He gets violent. I know it.' Mairéad stubbed out a cigarette and drained her tea. 'Have you another drop? Thanks. I'll drink this up. Then I'd better be going. I've been going on too much. It could be worse. You don't have to tell me. Wasn't my sister's boy shot? Killed outright. He was barely fourteen and the army said they thought he was a sniper. I ask you how could anyone take a fourteen-year-old for a sniper? You're from the south? I suppose all this is strange to you? I'm supposed to be here to get away from it all. You look forward to doing that and then the funny thing is you can't. It's as well I missed Rosheen. No point upsetting her, is there? You'll remember what I said to say, won't you? Thanks for the tea.'

Maggy saw her out and watched her walk away, turning, as she put distance between them, into a typical Irish charwoman such as you saw walking in their domesticated multitudes around the streets of Camden.

Dizzy, who got home before Rosheen, said: 'Don't mention the visit to her.'

'Mightn't she be glad to get the message?'

'Really, Maggy!' Dizzy sounded like a head girl – had *been* head girl when they were at school together, in spite or perhaps because of being the only Protestant. 'You have no sense of people,' she scolded. 'Rosheen has no sense at all.'

Maggy began to laugh at this arrogance and Dizzy – which was the nice thing about her – joined in. 'Seriously though,' she drove home her point. 'Rosheen could easily go back to that ghastly Sean. Just *because* he's so ghastly. She has to be protected from herself! From that Irish death wish. Surely you can see that she's better off with me.'

'With us?'

'With me. Don't be obtuse.'

Dizzy had been bossing Maggy and Rosheen since the day they'd met her. They'd all been about twelve at the time. Maggy knew this because she remembered that she and Rosheen had been on their way back to the convent after winning medals for under thirteens at a Feis Ceol. Maggy's was for verse-speaking and Rosheen's for Irish dance. Suddenly Rosheen let out a screech.

'I've lost me medal. What'll I do? The nuns'll be raging. They all prayed for me to win it and now I haven't got it to show.'

'It's winning that matters,' Maggy tried to soothe her. 'The medal isn't valuable. Come on. We'll miss our bus.'

'I'm not moving from this spot till I make sure I've lost it.'

Rosheen began to frisk herself. They were standing on a traffic island in the middle of O'Connell Street and it wasn't long before her manoeuvres began to attract attention. When she unbuttoned her vest to grope inside it, a tripper with an English accent shouted: 'Starting early, aren't you? What are you doing, love? Giving us a bit of a striptease?'

Maggy spat at him. It was an odd, barbaric gesture but, remembering, she could again feel the fury of the convent girl at the man's violation of dignity and knew her rage could not have been vented with less. Give her a knife and she'd have stuck it in him. The man must have seen insanity in her face for he wiped the spittle from his lapel and moved silently away. Rosheen, typically, had failed to notice the incident.

'I've lost it,' she decided, buttoning her blouse. 'I'm going to pray to Saint Anthony to get it back for me.' She knelt on the muddy pavement of the traffic island. 'Kneel down and pray with me,' she invited Maggy.

'Here?' Maggy's voice shot upwards. 'You shouldn't be let out, Rosheen O'Dowd! You should be tied up. People are *looking* at you!' Being looked at was agony to Maggy at that time. 'Rosheen,' she begged. 'Get up. You're destroying your gym-slip. Please, Rosheen. I bet,' she invented desperately, 'it's against the law. We're obstructing traffic. *Rosheen!*'

But all Rosheen had to say was: 'You're full of human respect. Shame on you.' And she began blessing herself with gestures designed for distant visibility. Like a swimmer signalling a lifeguard, she was trying for Saint Anthony's attention. He was known to be a popular and busy saint.

'I'm off.' Maggy, unable to bear another second of this, stepped off the traffic island in front of the advancing wheels of a double-decker bus which stopped with a shriek of brakes.

'Are you trying to make a murderer out of me?' The driver jumped out to shake her by the shoulders. 'That's an offence,' he yelled. 'I could have you summonsed. In court. What's your name and address?'

'Magdalen Mary Cashin, Convent of the Daughters of Passion.'

'What's that? A nursery rhyme?' The man was angry. Passengers were hanging out of the bus, staring. 'Tell me your real name,' the man roared, 'or . . .'

Maggy ducked from his grasp, ran and, miraculously missing the rest of the traffic, made it to the opposite footpath.

'What's chasing you?' A girl of about her own age was staring inquisitively at her. 'You're from the Passion Convent, aren't you? I know the uniform. I may be coming next term.'

'You?' Maggy was alert for mockery. 'You're a Protestant.'

'Not really. My parents are, vaguely, I suppose – but how did you know?'

Maggy shrugged. 'It's obvious.'

'How? I'd better find out, hadn't I?' the girl argued. 'If I'm coming to your school?'

'You wouldn't be let come like that.'

'Like what?'

'Look at your skirt.' Maggy spoke reluctantly. She was still unsure that she was not being laughed at. 'And you've no stockings on! Then there's your hair . . .' She gave up. The girl was hardly a girl at all. Protestants almost seemed to belong to another sex. Their skirts were as short as Highlanders' kilts and their legs marbled and blue from exposure. 'Don't you feel the cold?' she asked. Maybe Protestants didn't.

'No. I'm hardy. Do you wear vests and things? I despise vests and woolly knickers!'

The intimacy of this was offensive but Maggy's indignation had been so used up in the last ten minutes that her responses were unguarded.

'I do too but I'm made to wear them,' she said and felt suddenly bound to the person to whom she had made such a private admission.

'My name's Dizzy,' said Dizzy. 'Is that your friend over there? I think she's signalling.'

'She's odd.' Maggy disassociated herself from the embarrassing Rosheen, who was indeed waving and rising and replunging to her knees. 'Don't mind her,' she begged. 'It's best to pay her no attention.'

'She's praying, isn't she? That's marvellous.'

'What?'

'She doesn't give a damn. Catholicism interests me,' Dizzy confided. 'I think Catholics are more Irish, don't you?'

'More Irish than whom?'

'Us.'

'You?'

'We *are* Irish, you know,' Dizzy argued. 'My family has been here since the time of Elizabeth the First. They're mentioned in heaps of chronicles.'

That, to Maggy's mind, only showed how foreign they were. The chronicles would have been written by the invaders. But she didn't mention this. What interested her about Dizzy was not her likeness to herself but her difference. It was clear that she lacked the layers of doubt and caution which swaddled Maggy's brain as thickly as the unmentionable vests and bloomers did her body.

'I found it!' Rosheen had arrived, all pant and spittle. She waved the medal excitedly. 'Saint Anthony answered my prayer. I knew he would. Isn't he great?' Rosheen always spoke of saints as though they were as close to her as her dormitory mates. 'Do you know where I found it? You'll never believe me: in my shoe.'

'This is Rosheen O'Dowd,' said Maggy formally. 'I'm Margaret Mary Cashin and you're . . .?' She was chary of the ridiculous name.

'Dizzy,' said Dizzy. 'Desdemona FitzDesmond actually, but it's a mouthful, isn't it? So, Dizzy.'

'We're orphans,' Maggy thought to say.

'What luck,' said Dizzy. 'Wait till you meet my sow of a mother. She leads poor Daddy a dreadful dance. Drink, lovers, debts,' she boasted. 'Family life isn't all roses, I can tell you.'

The orphans were interested and impressed.

'Here's your tea.' The screw had brought a fresh tray. 'You'd be well advised to have it. As well start as you plan to finish and, believe me, they all eat in the end! Chips this evening,' she said.

Maggy smelled and imagined the pith of their insides and the crisply gilded shells. An ideal potato chip, big as a blimp, filled her mind's sky. The door closed; a rattle of keys receded down the corridor. Heels thumped. Teeth in other cells would be sinking through crisp-soft chips. Tongues would be propelling the chewed stuff down throats. If the din of metal were to let up she would surely hear soft munching. Her own saliva tasted salty. Or was it sweat? Did they count the chips put in her tray? Wouldn't put it past them. Tell us is she weakening. Keep count. They'd never. Wouldn't they just? Besides, to eat even one would surely make her feel worse.

There was no political status in England. No political prisoners at all. So why insist on treatment you couldn't get? They had made this point laboriously to her, then given up trying to talk sense to someone who wouldn't listen. People had died recently from forced feeding so they were chary of starting that. They followed the Home Secretary's Guidelines and what happened next was no skin off their noses. The country had enough troubles without worrying about the bloody Irish. Always whining and drinking, or else refusing to eat and blaming the poor old UK for all their woes. They had their own country now but did that stop them? Not on your nelly, it didn't. They were still over here in their droves taking work when a lot of English people couldn't find it. Rowdy, noisy. Oh forget it. When you saw all the black and brown faces, you almost came to like the Paddies if only they'd stop making a nuisance of themselves.

A man had come to see her, a small man with a glass eye whom she'd seen twice in Dizzy's flat. He was from the IRA. He winked his real eye while the glass one stared at her. He had claimed to be a relative, managing somehow to get visiting privileges. She must play along with his story, winked the eye. Was she demanding political status? Good.

'They'll deny it but we have to keep asking. It's the principle of the thing.'

There had been a confusion about him as though he didn't know whom to distrust most: her, himself, or the screws. His dead eye kept vigil and it occurred to her that one half of his face mistrusted the other.

Impossible to get comfortable. Her body felt as if enclosed in an orthopaedic cast. She had a sense of plaster oozing up her nose and felt tears on her cheeks but didn't know why she was crying, unless from frustration at the way she had boxed herself in like a beetle in a matchbox. She was boxed in by her ballady story. It didn't fit her, was inaccurate but couldn't be adjusted, making its point with the simple speed of a traffic light or the informative symbol on a lavatory door. She was in a prison within a prison: the cast. Slogans were scrawled on it: graffiti. She was a public convenience promenading promises to blow, suck, bomb the Brits, logos, addresses of abortion clinics, racial taunts. 'Wipe out all Paddies and nignogs now!' shrieked one slogan cut deep into her plaster cast inside which she wasn't sure she was. Maybe she'd wiped herself out?

She had committed a murder. Performed an execution. Saved a man's life.

Depending on how you looked at it. Who had? Maggy the merciful murderess.

Her story was this: she had been an orphan, her mother probably a whore. Brought up by nuns, she had lost her faith, found another, fought for it and been imprisoned. This was inexact but serviceable. If they made a ballad about it, Rosheen could sing it in a Camden pub.

When she was very small the nuns told Maggy that she had forty mothers: their forty selves. An aunt, visiting from Liverpool, was indignant.

'Frustrated old biddies!' These, she asserted, were mock mothers. 'You have your own,' she said. 'What are they trying to do? Kill her off? What do they know of the world?' she asked. 'Cheek.'

'What world?' Maggy wondered. She was maybe four.

'Now don't *you* be cheeky,' said the aunt.

On what must have been a later visit the aunt reported the mother to be dead. Maggy remembered eating an egg which must have been provided for consolation.

'I'll bet they'll say it's for the best,' raged the aunt and began painting her face in a small portable mirror. 'You didn't love her at all, did you?' she interrogated, moistening her eyelash brush with spit. 'I told her not to send you here. She'd have kept you by her if she could. Children,' the aunt said, 'have no hearts.'

The aunt too must have died for she didn't come back – and indeed maybe 'aunt' and 'mother' were one and the same? Maggy, when she grew older, guessed herself to be illegitimate, as there had never been any mention of a father. And so it proved when eventually she came to London and applied for a birth certificate to Somerset House.

'You don't know your luck. No beastly heritage to shuck off!'

Dizzy had come to the nuns' school to spite her mother who favoured agnosticism, raw fruit, fresh air and idleness for girls.

'Not that it matters where she goes to school!' The mother was mollified by the smallness of the nuns' fee. 'Nobody of my blood ever worked,' she said. 'Dizzy will marry young.' She spoke without force for she was to die of diabetes when Dizzy was fourteen. After that Dizzy's father became very vague and did not protest when she became a Catholic. Thus fortified, she was allowed by the nuns to invite Maggy home for weekends.

They spent these talking about what they took to be sex and dressing up in colonial gear which they found in the attic. Much of it was mildewed and so stiff that it seemed it must have been hewn rather than tailored. There were pith helmets and old-fashioned jodhpurs shaped like hearts. Dizzy's father had served in Africa, although she herself had been born after his return to Ireland when her mother was forty-four.

'I'm a child of the Change,' she relished the phrase. 'I'm not like them.'

Who she wanted to be like was the bulk of the local population, and, on Poppy Day, she hauled down the Union Jack which her father had raised. He was apologetic but this only annoyed her the more for she felt that he ought to have known his own mind. Dizzy was eager for order and when she became a Catholic fussed unfashionably about hats in church and fish on Fridays.

On leaving school, Maggy won a scholarship to an American university. Coming back, after eight years there, she met Dizzy again in London. This was a Dizzy who seemed to have lost much of her nerve for she blushed when Maggy asked: 'Did you know I was in love with you when we were in our teens?'

This was a requiem for someone no longer discernible in Dizzy, whom Maggy recalled as pale and volatile as the fizz on soda water. Dizzy had had fly-away hair worn in a halo as delicate as a dandelion clock. Her skin might have been blanched in the dusk of her secretive house. Agile and seeming boyish to Maggy who knew no boys, she swung up trees like a monkey so that one could see all the way up her skirt. She was Maggy's anti-self. Once, in a spirit of scientific inquiry, they showed each other their private parts. Later, Dizzy discovered this to be a sin or at least the occasion of one.

'You knew,' she accused. 'You should have told me.'

Maggy was disappointed to find freedom so fragile and each felt let down.

Now Dizzy's skin was opaque, thickish. She had lost her charm, but Maggy, although she might not have liked her if they'd just met for the first time, was responsive to memory. She felt linked by a bond she could not gauge to this woman who had first alerted her to the possibility of frankness. Dizzy had provided a model of mannish virtue at a time when Maggy knew no men and now Maggy, who had lost and left a man in America, found herself eager for support. Dizzy could still act with vigour. Look at the way she had rescued Rosheen.

The two – Maggy had heard the story from each separately – had not met for years when one night, a little over a year ago, they sat opposite each other on the North London underground. Rosheen's eyes were red; she had just run out of the house after being kicked in the stomach by Sean. For want of anywhere to go, she was heading for a late-night cinema.

'Leave him,' said Dizzy, 'you can stay in my flat.'

'I love him,' Rosheen told her. 'He needs me. He can't cope by himself. Poor Sean! He's gentle most of the time and when he's not, it's not his fault. He's sick, you see. His mother warned me: Mairéad. It's his nerves. Ulcers. Anyway we're married.'

'All the more reason,' Dizzy told her, 'to get out while you can. Are you going to have kids with a chap like that? You should call the police,' she lectured.

'I couldn't.' Rosheen was an underdog to the marrow.

'I could.' Dizzy had Anglo-Irish assurance. 'Just let him come looking for you.' She herded Rosheen home to her flat and the husband, when he presented himself, was duly given the bum's rush. He took to ambushing Rosheen, who went back to him twice but had to slink back to Dizzy after some days with black eyes and other more secret ailments.

'You're like a cat that goes out on the tiles,' Dizzy told her. 'You need an interest. You should come to political rallies with me.'

When Maggy arrived in London and agreed to move in with the two, Rosheen was working as an usherette in a theatre where Dizzy was stage manager. The plays put on by the group were revolutionary and much of Dizzy's conversation echoed their scripts.

'You have a slave mind,' she said without malice to Maggy, who claimed she was too busy finishing a thesis to have time for politics. Dizzy did not ask the subject of the thesis – it was semiology – nor show any interest in the years Maggy had spent in America. Having gathered that there had been some sort of man trouble, she preferred to know no more. To Rosheen, who showed more curiosity, Maggy remarked that her situation was much like Rosheen's own.

'Convalescing?'

'Yes.'

'This is a good place to do it,' said Rosheen. 'Though I sometimes think I won't be able to stand it. Sean keeps ringing me up. Crying. And I'm in dread that I'll break down and go back to him. I miss him at night something awful.'

'So why . . .'

'Ah sure it'd never be any good.'

'Is that what Dizzy tells you?'

'Yes. But sure I know myself that when a relationship has gone bad there's no mending it.'

'Relationship' would be Dizzy's word. But Maggy wasn't going to interfere. Rosheen she remembered from their childhood as unmodulated and unskinned: an emotional bomb liable to go off unpredictably. Better let Dizzy handle her. She herself was trying to finish her thesis before her money ran out. She spent her days at the British Museum, coming home as late as nine p.m. Often a gust of talk would roar into the hallway as she pushed open the door. 'Bourgeois crapology,' she'd hear, or: 'It's bloody *not* within the competence of the minister. Listen, I know the 1937 constitution by heart. D'ya want to bet?' The voices would be Irish, fierce and drunk. Maggy would slip into the kitchen, get herself food as noiselessly as she could manage and withdraw into her room. Towards the evening's end, Rosheen's voice invariably reached her, singing some wailing song and Maggy would have wagered any money that the grief throbbing through it had not a thing to do with politics.

Sometimes, the phone in the hall would ring and Rosheen would have it off the hook before the third peal. It was outside Maggy's bedroom door and she could hear Rosheen whisper to it, her furtive voice muffled by the coats which hung next to it and under which she seemed to plunge her head to hide perhaps from Dizzy.

'You're drunk,' she'd start. 'You are. Sean, you're not to ring here, I told you. I suppose they've just shut the pub . . . it's not that, no . . . even if you were cold stone sober I'd say the same . . . Listen, why don't you go to bed and sleep it off? Have you eaten anything? What about your ulcer? Listen, go and get a glass of milk somewhere . . . you can . . . I can't . . . it's not that. I do. I do know my own mind but . . . She's not a dyke, Sean . . . You know as well as I do it'd never work . . . If only you'd take the cure . . . Well it's a vicious circle then, isn't it? . . . Please, Sean, ah don't be that way, Sean . . . I do but . . . ah Sean . . .'

Sooner or later there would be the click of the phone. Rosheen would stand for a while among the coats, then open the door to go into the front room. Later, she would be singing again, this time something subdued like one of the hymns which they had sung together in school. This tended to put a damper on the party and the guests would clatter out shortly afterwards.

Next day smells of stale beer and ash pervaded the flat, and Rosheen's voice, raised in the shower, pierced through the slap of water to reach a half-sleeping Maggy.

> Mo-o-other of Christ,
> Sta-a-ar of the sea,
> Pra-a-ay for the wanderer.
> Pray for me.

'You missed a good evening,' Dizzy reproached. 'I don't know why you can't be sociable. Mix. There were interesting, committed people there. One was a fellow who escaped from Long Kesh.'

'I have reading to do.'

'Piffle! Do you good to get away from your books. Live. Open yourself to new experiences.'

The man Maggy had lived with in San Francisco had made similar reproaches. Books, he said, made Maggy egocentric. Squirrelling away ideas, she was trying to cream the world's mind. His was a sentient generation, he told her, but she reminded him of the joke about the guy caught committing necrophilia whose defence was that he'd taken the corpse to be a live Englishwoman.

'Irish.'

Irish, English – what was the difference? It was her coldness which had challenged him. He was a man who relished difficulty. Beneath her cold crust he'd counted on finding lava and instead what he'd found inside was colder still: like eating baked Alaska. Maggy, feeling that she was in violation of some emotional equivalent of the Trade Descriptions Act, blamed everything on her First Communion. She'd been rejected by her maker, she explained, thrown on the reject heap and inhibited since. This mollified her lover and they took an affectionate leave of each other. Now, in wintry London, where men like him were as rare as humming birds, she groaned with afterclaps of lust.

Well, if her thaw was untimely, the fault was her own.

What was really too bad was that Rosheen, who had passed the First Communion test with flying colours, should be unable to consummate her punctual passions. She was slurping out feeling now, steaming and singing in the shower while the other two ate breakfast.

'*Mother of Chri-i-ist* . . .'

'How was your First Communion?' Maggy asked Dizzy. 'Did you experience ecstasy?'

'I don't think anyone mentioned the word. I thought of it more as a way of joining the club. As a convert, you know.'

'*Sta-a-a-r of the* . . . Fuck!' Rosheen had dropped the shampoo. Now they would all get glass splinters in their feet.

'Didn't you notice the prayers?' Maggy wondered. '*May thy wounds be to me food and drink by which I may be nourished, inebriated and overjoyed!* Surely you remember that? And: *Thou alone will ever be my hope, my riches, my delight, my pleasure, my joy . . . My fragrance, my sweet savour?* It goes on.'

'Do you think bloody Rosheen's cut herself? It's a responsibility having her around. I didn't think you were pious, Maggy. More toast?'

'I saw it all,' said Maggy, 'as a promise of what I'd find outside the convent: men like Christs who'd provide all that.'

'I do think semiology is the wrong thing for you, Maggy. You should put your energies into something practical.'

'Dizzy, you're a treat! You've been trying to de-Anglicize yourself since the day we met, but your officer-class genes are too much for you.'

This was going too far. Dizzy, hurt, had to be sweetened by a gift of liqueur jam for which Maggy had to go all the way to Harrods. The trip made her late and when she got back to the flat Dizzy had left for the local pub. Maggy, joining her there, found her chatting to a man who sometimes dropped in after work. He was a sandy-haired chap who probably worked in an insurance office. Dizzy imagined him as starved for life and in search of anecdotes. 'I drop into an Irish pub in Camden,' he would tell his wife who would be wearing an apron covered with Campari ads. Dizzy, nourishing this imagined saga, had tried to get Rosheen to sing while he was in the pub, though it was always too early and the ambience wasn't right. 'It *is* an IRA pub, you know,' she had told him, slipping in and out of Irishness as though it were stage make-up.

'I believe less and less in democracy,' she was saying when Maggy arrived. 'Hullo, Maggy. What're you having? Don't you agree that democracy is a con? Do you know who said "the people have no right to do wrong"? Also "there are rights which a minority may justly uphold in arms against a majority"? Bet you don't.'

The man in the belted mac and sandy hair had nothing to say to this. Dizzy, however, could carry on two ends of a conversation.

'You might say,' she supplied, 'that the people have a right to decide for themselves. But "the people" are people like that gutless wonder, Sean. *They* never initiate change, so . . .'

Maggy left for the loo. Through its window she saw Sean and Rosheen embracing in the damp and empty garden of the pub. Both seemed to be crying. It might, however, be rain on their cheeks. She went back to the lounge.

'Saw it in Malaya,' the macintoshed man was saying. 'Bulk of the people were loyal. Just a few agitators. You've got to string 'em up right at the start. Cut off the gangrened limb. Else you'll have chaos.'

'But I,' said Dizzy, 'was speaking *on behalf* of the agitators, the leaven, the heroes!'

'Oh,' the man moved his glass away from hers. 'I could hardly go along with that.'

Rosheen stood at the door of the lounge and beckoned Maggy behind Dizzy's back. She put a finger on her lips.

'I'm going.' Maggy got up.

Rosheen rushed Maggy down a corridor. 'Let's get out of here. That man's in the Special Branch. A detective. He's looking for Sean.'

'Why . . . but then Dizzy . . .?'

'Dizzy's an eejit, doesn't know whether she's coming or going.'

'You think Dizzy's an eejit?' Maggy couldn't have been more astonished if a worm had stood erect on its tail and spoken.

'You know she is, Maggy! She's in way over her head. Wait till I tell you.' Rosheen's eyes were red, but she spoke lucidly. 'It's Sean they're after. They want him to turn informer and if he doesn't, they'll spread the word that he *has*. Then the I R A will get him. And you know what *they* do to informers.'

'Are you sure?' Maggy asked, but it was likely enough. She remembered Mairéad's description of the nerve-shot Sean. He was the very stuff of which the police could hope to make an informer. His family had a record. Had he one himself? 'Is he political?' she asked.

'No, but they could nail him. They can nail anyone.'

'But what does he *know*? I mean what information has he?'

'That's the trouble,' Rosheen told her. 'He doesn't know much at all. But in self-defence he'll have to shop someone and the only one he can think of is Dizzy.'

'Dizzy?'

'You see she's not real I R A: only on the fringe, expendable. Sean thinks they mightn't mind about her. The I R A, I mean. And naturally *he* hates her.' Rosheen blushed and added quickly, 'This is killing him. He's passing blood again. Both sides have their eye on him now. He's been seen talking to that detective, so if anything at all happens in the next few weeks, it'll be blemt on Sean. I think he's a dead man.' Rosheen spoke numbly. 'If one lot doesn't get him, the others will.'

'And what *is* Dizzy up to? I mean what could he tell them?'

Rosheen turned stunned eyes on Maggy, who saw that there was no turning *her* into an Emerald Pimpernel. Dizzy, having stumbled onto territory which Rosheen knew better, might be revealed as an eejit and a play-actress but Rosheen herself, helpless as a heifer who has somehow strayed onto the centre divider of a highway, could only wait and wonder whether the traffic of events might be miraculously diverted before it mowed her down. 'What do they get expendable people like her to do?' she asked. 'Plant bombs.'

Dizzy, when faced with the question, reacted violently: 'Maggy, are you working for the Special Branch? Shit, I should have known! All that pretence at being apathetic – or,' her eyes narrowed, 'is it Rosheen who's been talking? I always thought Sean had the stuff of a stool pigeon.' She went on like this until Maggy cut her short with the news that who *was* in the Special Branch was Dizzy's drinking companion whose phone number Maggy – thanks to Rosheen – was in a position to let her have.

'It's a Scotland Yard number. Check if you like,' she said, astounded at the way Dizzy's authority had crumbled. It was like the emperor's clothes: an illusion, nothing but RADA vowels, that officer-class demeanour, thought Maggy, who now felt powerful and practical herself. Rosheen, like one of those creatures in folk tales who hand the heroine some magic tool, had made Maggy potent.

In return, the helper must herself be helped. Maggy remembered Rosheen's telephone colloquies with Sean seeping, regularly as bedtime stories, under her own bedroom door and that Rosheen's renunciatory voice had quavered like a captive bird's as she hid among the heavy coats in Dizzy's front hall. Now she must be allowed to unleash her precarious passion in peace.

'*You're* a security risk, you must see that,' said Maggy to Dizzy, making short work of her protests. 'So you'd better let me pick up your bomb. Never mind why I want to. That's my concern. Motives,' she told her, 'are irrelevant to history. If I do this for the IRA, I shall be IRA. Wasn't that your own calculation?'

This bit of rhetoric proved truer than foreseen, for a number of squat, tough-faced, under-nourished-looking people turned up at her trial and had to be cleared from the public gallery where they created a disturbance and gave clenched-fist salutes. They seemed to have co-opted her act, and her lawyer brought along copies of excitable weekly papers which described it in terms she could not follow because their references were rancorous and obscure. One was called *An Phoblacht*, another *The Starry Plough* and there was a sad daily from Belfast full of ads for money-lenders, in memoriam columns and, for her, a bleak fraternity. Dizzy did not come and neither did Rosheen.

Who did attend the trial and visit her afterwards was the glass-eyed man. 'All Ireland is with you,' he said, 'all true Irish Socialist Republicans.' Was this a joke? Did the eye gleam with irony? Or had he meant that her act was public property, whether she liked this or not, and despite the fact that her victim had not been Dizzy's target at all? *That* was to have been a building and there was to have been a telephone warning to avoid loss of life. Maggy thought this ridiculous. A war was a war and everyone knew how those warnings went wrong. The police delayed acting so as to rouse public feeling against the bombers – for how much anger could be generated if explosions hurt nobody, going off with the mild bang of a firework display? Property owners would be indignant, but the police needed wider support than theirs. Yes, the police were undoubtedly the culprits. They bent rules. Detective Inspector Coffee had been bending rules when he told the nerve-shot Sean that he'd put the word about in Irish pubs that Sean was an informer unless he became one. An old police trick! It had landed men in a ditch with a bullet in the neck before now. How many had Detective Inspector Coffee nudged that way? How many more would he? None, because Maggy had got him with Dizzy's bomb.

'For personal reasons,' she told Glass Eye.

'It's *what* you did that counts.'

What she had done astounded her. She had been like one of those mothers who find the sudden strength to lift lorries and liberate their child. Unthinkingly, almost in a trance, she had phoned the number given her by Rosheen and asked for an appointment. She had information of interest, she promised, and evidence to back it up. Could she bring it round at once? Where she'd got the number? Oh, please, she didn't want to say this on the phone. '*They* may be listening, watching. Maybe I'm paranoid but I've got caught up in something terrifying. By chance.'

Her genuinely shaky voice convinced him and he proved more

guileless than she could have believed for she had gone to the meeting fearful of being frisked by attendant heavies. But no. There were no preliminaries. She got straight to the man himself.

'Detective Inspector Coffee?'

He was the sandy-haired chap all right. Perhaps he had recognized her voice on the phone? She handed him a bag. There were documents on top of the device which was primed to go off when touched.

'I brought you papers. You'll see what they are. I'm afraid I'm a bit rattled. Nausea. Could I find a loo?'

He showed her the way, then walked back into his room. She was two flights down the stairs, when she heard the explosion. Oddly – she had expected her fake nausea to become real – she felt nothing but elation. There were shattering noises, shouts, a bell. She thought: that's put an end to his smile, his assurance, his smug, salary-drawing, legal murder. The word registered then and, seeing him in her mind's eye blown apart, she began to sweat. The smell was pungent when she reached the outer door where a policeman stopped her.

'You'll demand political status?' asked the glass-eyed man. 'Go on hunger strike until they grant it.'

'Political?'

He was impatient, the visit nearly over. A group in another wing of the prison were all set to strike. He was planning publicity which would have more impact if she joined in. 'Listen, love,' he said, 'you're political or what are you?'

Political? The notion exhilarated. Old songs. Solidarity. We shall overcome. In gaol, as in church, that sort of language seemed to work. On a snap decision, she agreed and, in after-image, the gleam of his eye pinned her to the definition. As she grew weaker, her weathercock mind froze at North-North-East. The strike gave purpose to her days and, like the falling sparrow's, her pain became a usable statistic. 'Get involved,' commanded an ad in the *Irish News* which the glass-eyed man brought on a subsequent visit. '*They* did.' A list of hunger-strikers included Maggy's name.

Her mind was flickering. Sharp-edged scenes faltered and she wondered whether thin people like herself had less stamina than others. It was too soon, surely, to be so weak? She had a fantasy –

some of the time it was a conviction – that her lover from San Francisco had come and that they had done together all the things she – no: he – had always wanted to do. Like a drowning person's flash vision of a lifetime, a whole erotic frieze unrolled with convincing brilliance in her mind. Sensory deprivation was supposed to make you hallucinate, she remembered, but confused this false prison visitor with real ones. His eyes gleamed like glass. 'Sentient,' he had said of himself and 'cold' of her, but her memory of him was bright like ice and cold. She *was* cold. It was part of her condition. And her mouth was dry. In her fantasy – or reality? – he offered her an icicle to suck.

'Don't talk,' said someone, 'save your saliva.'

Now her lover was lying naked and wounded beside her and offered her his wounds to moisten her lips, but they too were dry and not as food and drink to her at all.

Vitamins and hormones were being used up.

This was the prison doctor talking now. He had checked her blood and urine and felt it his duty to warn her that irreversible effects could occur.

'Jaundice,' warned the doctor.

'Golden, gilded skin,' said her lover. 'Here,' he presented her with a golden potato chip. 'Eat this for me.'

'Eat,' said the screw.

'Do yourself a favour,' said the doctor.

Maggy put the chip in her mouth. It was dry. She couldn't swallow it. It revived her nausea.

Oh My Monsters!

It's freakish! Appalling! I can't bear to think about it!

Thoughts forward.

To whom or what? Oh, to whom but Kiki. Yes, unknown to you, Kiki, I'm on my way. The train has pulled out of Paris-Lyon. Goodbye. Goodbye. The rural womb awaits. *Merde!* Now I've depressed myself and there's no one to cheer me. Minutes ago, a man stuck his head in the compartment door, paused, withdrew himself. Mustn't have liked what he saw. So here I'm on my own till Dijon with nary a buffer between me and me. Nothing but a litre of cognac and nembutal in the little malachite box given me by – never mind whom. Every item I possess has a name attached, so better not start the attributing game. What will I do then? Sing? Count sheep? Make up a limerick? A lady who loved to get laid – what rhymes with that? Well, there's 'renegade': that's me, ever ready to join a new army, sew fresh colours on my faded sleeve. My armies, Kiki, are my men and – since I too have my honour – I join one at a time and keep step with the current paymaster. Yessir! I'm loyal while I last, the perfect batwoman, quick to absorb new tastes and learn to shop within the confines of almost any budget. References aplenty. *Premier prix de souplesse:* I can operate in French, British and American, upper to lower – well, better say lower-middle – class arenas. *Parfaitement*, Kiki, and don't think apologies are intended. Either now or when we meet.

Look, if I take my style and world view from my current man and he his from his current job, whose integrity is weaker? Is it better to adapt for love or money? To embrace the values of the Rand Corp., the Quai d'Orsay or the Faculté de Philo of the

University of Grenoble? Or to embrace Rand etc. values through and in the person of a man?

I've no idea.

Truly. You see, Kiki, currently, I'm valueless, being manless, demobbed, out of uniform and with no reference points. The last ones turned out unreliable for the man was mad: a most disconcerting event. I wonder can you tell how disconcerting? No? Look, it was as though some executive were suddenly to learn that the corporation for which he worked did not exist, had been – say – a project cooked up by some well-funded psychologists eager to study executives' behaviour. After months – or years – of diligence on his part, they tell him 'it wasn't real', give him a golden handshake and let him go. Where does that leave him?

I wouldn't know. I've lost my criteria.

(She lost her *what*? Oh some little thing she had removed. Probably one of those feminine 'ops' so common after thirty.)

Jokes, Kiki, are getting unfunny. I'm in one, you see: the reason I never knew he was mad was that I thought he was being funny. Funny-haha, you know, but instead he was funny-peculiar. Doesn't it just kill you, Kiki. No, but it may me.

I wonder will you be glad or under strain when I turn up? I should, of course, have written – but some things are hard to get down on paper. I meant to. Really. I kept, keep, writing to you in my head.

'Dear' – goes my head-letter – 'Kiki, I do think about you. I mayn't write but I talk to you in my mind all the time. Well, "mind" is a word which makes me blush. I feel shame about using it of the place in which I spend my days and nights. It's a cerebral slum, a *louche* blue-movie house . . .'

Dear Kiki, the truth is I have no mind. That's why I can't answer your concerned and reasonable letters. You always said I hadn't. Remember? 'Anne-Marie,' you said, 'is alive from her waist down. As for her head . . .' You shrugged your hump. Your hump gave you prestige. It was something the rest of us didn't have. It put you out of the running for the marriage-market and, by extension, out of our sex. Your extra protuberance made a man of you. You were, even before Jacques, Papa and Gérard died, the true *chef de famille*.

We're in open country now: bare, frozen fields. The train zips over them, quick as a fly-zipper. A nip of brandy forward. I need support.

'I hope,' your last letter says, 'this marriage is not going to be another mistake. Tell me about Sam.'

Damn you, Kiki, you've made yourself my conscience. Do you know what the result has been? No, but I'll tell you. This time when we meet you're going to be told. It has meant that I've always left the job to you. Kiki has had the conscience, Anne-Marie the cunt-science. Oh weep tears of sperm and lubricant! I live in my cunt! You can't begin to imagine what it feels like, can you? Can't and wouldn't try. But this isn't a joke. Mentally I'm wound around, head between my own legs, eyes and brain swaddled in a monotonous cuntscape.

Apologia and quota of self-pity: another thing you can't imagine is what it's like to have to adjust to no longer trading on charm. At my age.

A hump-shrug here. I know. I know. Plain women have no patience with this plea, even take it for a kind of boast. You called me 'the dumb beauty' – but have you ever wondered why are dumb beauties dumb? Sister, the first reason is because they have no reason not to be and the second that the brain tuned to pleasure functions differently. Essential parts atrophy. Comes the day when it can only cope with dream. I think that's happened to mine, Kiki. When I'm woken up I panic. When I lose a man . . .

Over the last few years I've lost several. I'll tell you about one. Not Sam. A Greek who was very desirable, very grand and wanted to marry me. He changed his mind because I never emptied the ash-trays. It was a silly mistake but, you see, I wasn't tuned to the practical side of things. He was a sexually thrilling man. When we were together I could think of nothing but that and imagined that neither could he. We used to stay in bed all day, smoking; the ash from our cigarettes kept piling up and whenever a breeze blew in would sift around the room. It fell on our bed and he laughed and said we were like lovers in Pompeii and must make sure the lava would find us in the attitude of love. So we made love over and over while the curtain billowed in from the balconies like swollen sails or bridal veils and the ash circulated. It was June. We were staying at the Crillon. The weather was showery and, outside, the

Place de la Concorde was all hazy and bright: a Renoir canvas. He kept telling me he loved me and wanted his mother to meet me. Then we'd ring for room-service and have food sent up with more cigarettes. When his mother did come the place was like a disaster-area: mascara on the sheets, my hair a bird's nest, pairs of tights telescoped all over the floor. The flowers he had bought me had gone rank and there were apple-cores everywhere. She stood there looking astounded and all I could do was laugh. It was really a gasp – but I had no chance to explain. Terrible memory. Forget. Suppress. She would probably not have approved of me anyway so what the hell. Mothers never do. Neither do best friends, councils of responsible kin, etc., etc. That brigade has broken more of my engagements than I care to remember. They're the Fates, the Furies. I know once they're there I'm out. Sometimes they've offered me money. Sometimes I've had to accept it. Well what do you do if you're turfed off a cruise in Crete or Reykjavik?

It's – try and understand this, Kiki – the impinging, the crash-landing of one sort of reality on another. And does this make sense to you: when really grubby moments like that engulf me, I think of you. Maybe you're my stake in the world of family-values?

That world is constantly threatening to withdraw my residence-permit. Others' mothers issue those. Matrons. Sweet and ruthless. Marsha's the first who's ever liked me. I knew her before I did Sam. She introduced us.

'Hey Anne-Marie,' she said last week, 'I can't tell you what a kick it gives me that you're marrying Sam. I mean *we* get on so well! Now I know pleasing your mother-in-law is not the prime aim in marriage, but,' endearing laugh, endearing shrug, 'if it happens it's a bonus.'

Wait, Kiki, you'll see the irony of that later.

Marsha's from New York, boozy, a hairdresser's blonde and likes a good giggle. Also she's loaded.

Vulgar Anne-Marie! *Vulgaire!* I love that word: the first strongly charged one I learned. It's so dated now! Its frank snob-bery is, I suppose, vulgar in our devious days. I like your use of it: robust like the special corsets you get from your supplier in Annecy who claims his stock hasn't varied in forty years. But, darling, I'm really not vulgar, not even venal. I guy myself when I think of you but actually I'm disinterested. I'll do nothing for money. Not a thing. Oh – and maybe that's what worries you most? I imagine you worrying. You adjust your poultice, sip your gargle, spit it out and worry. Who is this man I'm marrying *now*? This Sam?

Sam? He's hard to pin down. Supply your own idea of 'attractive'. He's mine. He has that deadpan American humour which I don't always get. He'll say things like this: 'Know something, Anne-Marie? You're a double-nut! Why? Because you want to marry me and I – I'm telling you this up front – am a certified nut. Marsha had to smuggle me out of the States. They wanted to put my ass in the booby-trap. You thought I was dodging the draft, didn't you? Well what I was dodging was the nut-house. That means that for me to want to marry you is rational. A normal is an asset to a nut but the normal who marries a nut is behaving in an irrational manner, hence nuttier than the nut!'

We laughed. Christ, Kiki, I thought he was joking! More deadpan Yankee humour. Irony and all. Ha! More irony: your relief at hearing I was getting married again. I have your letter in my bag. It has grown soft as tissue from being carried there.

'I had begun to despair,' it says, 'of your ever settling down to a normal life . . . wondering how responsible we might be for the way you turned out. I suppose, since you were the youngest, we did spoil you and by spoil,' you elucidate, 'I mean "damage"!'

Oh Kiki, did you? How much? And how can I tell?

Several hours yet to Chambéry. Rows of poplars slide past, leafless, rasping the sky. I root in my over-night case for a valium. The case is in sealskin, carries the creams and colours of my identikit and is known to vulgar Parisiens as a *baise-en-ville*.

I thought of phoning you – but long-distance calls upset you. I imagined you in bed – it was six a.m. when I got the idea – and having to grope down two flights of uncarpeted stairs to the phone in the hall. Later, you would have been watching coffee on the kitchen stove. I saw it boil over, spattering onto the white enamel as you ran to take my call. After that you would go out to feed the hens and loose the dogs, slopping through muck in wellingtons which you would have to drag off, cursing genteel curses in the doorway then rushing to stop the phone's brash peal.

'*Crotte*,' you'd mutter, '*crotte de bique.*'

So I didn't ring. I'll just come.

'What's the matter?' you'll say. First thing. Braced, Anne-Marie means trouble, you think, has no sense, no head on her shoulders; sometimes you add 'no brains!'

This shouldn't annoy me but does. Every time. I was the only one in a family of seven sisters and one brother to pass the Baccalauréat – but somehow none of you was impressed. I am a paragraph-reader too and that counts against me. 'Skims the surface,' you say as you thumb your own laborious way down the columns of *La Croix*. When I do a long-division sum in my head, you react as though I'd done a conjuring trick: something not in the best of taste and whose reliability had better be checked. 'Remember,' you say ungenerously, 'the hare and the tortoise!' Haven't you heard, Kiki, this is the jet-age? Hares have been rehabilitated. Tortoises are out! Your yardstick is obsolete – not that I'd care, if only you wouldn't beat me with it. If only you wouldn't keep on about hoping I'll settle down to a 'normal' life. God, that dictatorial word. It's going to get between us, Kiki. It's going to make it hard for me to stay. Because I'm not going to sit around wearing penitential sackcloth admitting that every last thing I ever did was aberrant and that my failure confirms the authority of your norm.

Because, darling, there are more norms in the hexagon of France than you or I could imagine. Everyone thinks theirs is best. My ex-husband, Jean-Louis, couldn't see for a minute what I found wrong with his. As a *prof de philo*, he should, one might have thought, have known about relativities and things looking different from different angles and in different temperatures. I always felt he had a band of cold air around him and his tempo was decidedly not mine. I have a high metabolism which means I do things fast. I get bored fast too, but while I'm with a man I'm totally involved. Frighteningly: I have an impulse to die when I make love. That's why I keep the nembutal in the garage. These impulses wilt in the time it takes to get downstairs. I said this to Jean-Louis and he thought it in terrible taste. I remember him switching on the light and pulling away from me. He had a look of someone who's smelled gas and is worrying about the leak. He liked things mashed up in wordy abstractions. Then he could cope. He could cope with the most extreme notions once he'd put them into his abstract jargon, but by

67

then I'd be bored. Besides I never did learn his vocabulary. I remember complaining – jokingly – to our local grocer that I couldn't understand my husband's philosophisms. The grocer was very quick-witted and a whizz at crosswords. He had a café in his grocery and I used to sit there when I'd finished my shopping and we'd race each other through the day's crossword. He had a dictionary of philosophical terms which he'd got for doing this and he gave it to me to help me understand my husband. 'To promote understanding in family-life,' he said. I told Jean-Louis and he was furious – said I was making a fool of him in the village, that the grocer's nephew was in his class and that now all the pupils would be laughing behind his back. I couldn't see this at all. But then I never could see things Jean-Louis's way even after I had the dictionary. We moved to Grenoble shortly after that and he began teaching at the university and bringing a brilliant female student of his home for meals. She had very little money and needed feeding, he said. While I cooked, she and he used to talk about Althusser and Husserl and *épiphénomènes* and *épistémologie and épi*-this and *épi*-that and, though I kept the dictionary in the kitchen drawer, I could never remember which was which and used to get so furious that I would find myself putting sugar in the stew and chopping my finger into the parsley. He was sleeping with her of course and when I found out and said: OK, I hoped they'd enjoy each other and I was leaving, he couldn't understand at all. It was quite normal, he said, for me to be annoyed, but it was normal for him to have been drawn to her as a fellow searcher in the same field and really the carnal thing between them had been just a moment of tenderness, a kind of seal on their friendship and no more and his long-term commitment was to me and it was not normal for me to fail to see this or to throw all up for a moment's pique. Then he used one of his *épi*-words and I saw that the whole point of the jargon was to make very ordinary thinking seem grand and to camouflage the mean caution of his commitment to life in general and to me in particular. His favourite ordinary – non-jargon – word, Kiki, was 'normal'. I've been suspicious of it since. I met him some years later in a street in Saint Tropez and we had a drink for old time's sake. He said he had almost not recognized me and I, as one does, asked had I got so old and he said no but that in the old days I used to dress in a normal way whereas now . . . I roared with laughter.

'Jean-Louis,' I said. 'Look around you. This *is* the normal way. It's what everybody's wearing.'

It was summer and I was wearing a cheesecloth caftan and sandals. He looked around and most women were indeed wearing something like it. He kept looking and then, finally, a look of relief spread over his face. 'There's a normally dressed woman,' he said, nodding at a very provincial-looking girl in a pleated tartan skirt which was the wrong length for that year, a saddle-stitched bag and imitation-Gucci moccasins: the very sort of outfit I used to wear when I lived with him. I was suddenly very moved. My throat closed up with emotion and I wanted to put my arms around old Jean-Louis. I couldn't be sure: was I feeling this way because he'd made his 'norm' out of his memory of me and would be expecting brilliant *philo* students to conform to it forever more or because I realized that if I'd stayed with him I'd have gone on being a different person to the one I am now? I don't know. Anyway, a strong nostalgia for things past seized me and I felt quite lustful towards Jean-Louis, so I got up and left. I was living with someone else at the time and, as I've said, I am quite scrupulous about keeping my polyandry serial rather than simultaneous.

As for your norm, Kiki, it upsets me to think of it. But I do. I constantly think of you and our sisters mending your gumboots with bicycle-repair kits, hair scrunched into rain-bonnets, hands, stumpy as feet, reddened and ruined from trying to raise cash by selling chicken-shit, fruit and battery-hens. I see it all through a black frame like the edge on the mourning-cards you send me with such regularity that I could paper the loo with them: 'Pray for the soul of Aunt Madeleine-Sophie who died on this day fifteen years ago. R I P.' All our older relatives are dead. The younger and more robust left years ago for Egypt, Algeria or Indo-China, moved on when those places proved inhospitable, then failed to keep in touch. You are left with your commemorative cards and a few nuns who come out of their convents on name days and holy days to eat. As monastic rules relax, they come oftener, eat more and take back scraps in bags for friends less well provided for. They never bring you anything. I see you cooking for them, making meals from scratch – no meat-cube ever entered your kitchen. Labour has no value. Jean-Luc is set to churning the old ice-cream bucket, cranking it by hand for maybe an hour, then to pick flowers for the aunts to take back to their convent altars. Jean-Luc is fourteen now: the last surviving male in a family of females, the last child in a house whose ways were set when we were all in the nursery. Only he justifies them now. Your norm, my poor Kiki, will soon be quite bizarre. Norms, you see, are shifty.

I AM NORMAL!

I once typed that out on a postcard I'd happened to find in a drawer and considered sending you. The card was one of those plump, embroidered ones with a pressed edelweiss stuck on it and I must have bought it from a beggar at some resort. You might even have liked it although it had picked up a smell of stale cosmetics from lying so long in the drawer. But when I re-read the words they looked silly. The longer I looked, the shiftier they got. In the end the type seemed to be twitching like flies getting ready to do a bunk. Would anyone normal write such a thing?

Probably, I decided, it was the baldness of the statement that undermined it. It needed context, a bit of clutter. Like my life.

Clutter is ballast. You and my other sisters know that. You weight your lives with balls and bales of string, old knives, invitations to and reject gifts from other people's weddings. Do you remember, Kiki, that you kept every scrap of plate and silver I got for mine? For my first wedding which may well – brace yourself – be my only one. Admit that it provided a good haul! The family had been marriage-shy for so long that a fund of repossessed gifts had accumulated: objects whose owners had been removed by death or a monastic vocation. They were trotted out for my benefit, gift-wrapped with some flourish, presented with relief. Who can be bothered nowadays to clean silver? Answer: Kiki can.

'You keep it,' I told you. I knew you wanted it, had seen you touch the stuff as a timid shop-lifter might: fingers poised then retreating in an empty, hankering clench.

'Keep it all!' I said.

'You're mad!' you said, 'these are your *wedding presents*!'

'But I don't want them. Really. Sell them if you like, Kiki. They're yours.'

'But that's not *normal*!'

'I think it is. It seems quite normal to me.'

'Oh *you*!' You laughed. But you kept the silver.

Darling. I'm being querulous, fighting with you already in my head – and so why then am I coming back? Because Kiki, I'm at my lowest ebb, lost, lonely, maybe mad. Maybe. For the first time I could believe it.

'You,' said Sam yesterday, 'are a double nut . . .'

It appals me to think of his saying that. I told Rosemary – the girl I stayed with last night. She's known Sam for years.

'I thought,' I told her and kept crying as I tried to tell her, 'that it was a joke! You know the way Sam horses around!'

'Anne-Marie,' she said, 'he was trying to warn you. Sam's devious. Proud. He had to make a joke of it but you should have known it wasn't one. Anyone else would have! I mean – how long have you two lived together? Eight months? Well, surely then – I mean you must have wondered sometimes at his behaviour?'

'I thought he joked a lot.'

'Well he did,' said Rosemary, 'but nobody jokes all the time!'

Kiki, I'm trying to find ways to tell you – hell, there's no good way.

What about a telegram: *Engagement broken Sam gaoled. Stop. Arriving tonight. Stop. Anne-Marie.*

And stop and let me off. Sam drove through a red light yesterday shortly after telling me of his and my nuttiness. We were on our way to the country to stay with Rosemary and her husband whose name is Dirk and who was at Johns Hopkins with Sam. Sam was in a chatty mood.

'Weddings,' he told me, 'are a collective celebration of blood-letting, human sacrifice and the offering of virgins – *en principe*, virgins,' here he pinched my crotch with his gear-shifting hand, 'so as to further the increase of the clan. Barbarous survivals. White veils, for God's sake! Rice! Old shoes. Will you wear a white veil, Anne-Marie, to commemorate all the white lambs sacrificed to the rite? Or a black one? Let's make our wedding recognisably monstrous. Let's invite the world's worst monsters.'

'Who are they?' I was looking out the window at a passing turnip field.

'Nixon, Ron Reagan, Shirley Temple Black.' Sam reads the *Herald Tribune* every day and his hell is entirely North American.

'Where will you get them? From the waxworks?' A Citroën raced past slick as a wet cockroach. The whole of the Route Nationale 7 was slick. I was only half listening but could tell that Sam was still sounding off in some abstract way. I turned to look at him.

He's twenty-nine and I'm thirty-five and my mind tends to get stuck in the implications of that. Worry about my shortcomings – cellulite in the thigh, morning puffiness about the eye – kept me from wondering was there anything the matter with him. You see I'm used to being the flawed one, the one on trial and this time I was supposed to be the judge – naturally, I never realized it.

'Will you get your monsters from the waxworks?' I asked him.

'I'm going to invite the originals,' he said and put his foot on the accelerator. It was a good road but we were already going too fast. 'I'm inviting Nixon and Spiro Agnew to our wedding,' he said. 'Colonel Amin and Roman Polanski. Oh and the Chilean junta.'

I was tired of the joke. Maybe because the speedometer was still climbing. 'Don't you think,' I suggested, 'that they might be too busy to attend?'

Something hard and heavy landed on my mouth. It was his fist which he'd flung sideways. His ring split my lip. My neck wrenched backwards and I saw everything dark for moments with two swoops of concentric circles like luminous eyes – my own I suppose – glaring at me out of the blackness like flicked-up headlights.

'Don't contradict me!' yelled Sam.

The speedometer was at a hundred. The car wove across a miraculously empty road.

'I'm sorry,' I apologized swiftly. 'I was joking.'

'Don't you joke with me!'

'No,' I gabbled cravenly, 'no, no I won't.' There was blood in my mouth. I tested my teeth. They seemed steady. However, my tongue felt odd and my lip was swelling. I tried to think of something soothing to say. He was, it came to me in a lucid flash, a Super-Maniac. A joker in the pack, he had appeared as King of Hearts but instead was the Knave: kinkiness itself, the epitome of all male trickery. I'd known other freaks but Sam was the worst. He had given no warning. After eight months as the perfect lover, he was now, like a flipped card, showing his other face. I knew. At once. People find this odd – Dirk and Rosemary did – that I should have gone on so long having no suspicion of him then have realized at one blow. But I did. It was like that. He was, I knew then, Nemesis sent by some Dark Venus to punish me.

'We'll invite Solzhenitsyn,' Sam yelled.

'OK,' I shouted. 'As you like. Anything.'

The speedometer dropped and we made it to Dirk and Rosemary's. Thank God it was them. Half an hour after we'd sat down to drinks and chat, Sam – I can remember no provocation leading up to this – put down his vodka, walked to where I was sitting, knocked me out of my chair and began to kick me. Dirk was on him in a second. He's stronger than Sam and had him off me at once. It was all suspiciously smooth.

'You *knew*!' I challenged Rosemary in the bathroom.

She handed me cold-cream and tissues. 'What?'

'Sam's a nut-case! *Dingue!* Why did nobody tell me?' I was crying.

'It wasn't our business to tell you, but, yes, he's been committed several times. His mother . . .'

'Yes?'

'She hoped you'd cure him. He's been all right for a long while.'

'You mean nobody would have told me? At any point?'

Rosemary managed to look conniving but remote. She and Dirk are Sam's friends. After all. Fellow-Americans in France. To them *I*'m the foreigner.

'Look,' she excused, 'we supposed you'd guessed. Something . . . Besides, we weren't sure you really meant to marry him. You might have been playing along with his fantasies – joking.' Conciliatingly, she offered me a packet of Wash 'n' Dries.

Later she said, 'You'd better spend the night here.'

She went off to cook. Dirk had managed to get Sam out of the house. I'd heard the car leave. For where? I suppose I was only now feeling the shock. I sat in Rosemary's drawing-room and drank Kirs. One Kir after another, mixing them solemnly myself, pouring the clammy red drops of Cassis in various doses into glasses of cold white wine. Blood-thick at first, they dissolved in a faint blush, a memory of sweetness in the dryness. I hadn't drunk Kirs since leaving Jean-Louis. It had been our drink. In England I got onto

Scotch. With Sam – oh shit and *merde*! I smashed down a glass and two pink drops jumped out of it.

'I'm sending you,' you wrote last year, 'two cases of Papa's 1952 wine. His own. We found it in the lower cellar behind a vat which had got stuck and . . .'

I knew you wanted something from me. Of course.

'Poor Lucette's boy, Jean-Luc, is thirteen. He's running wild,' you wrote, 'around here. I'm afraid he'll end up like poor Jacques . . .'

Poor, poor, poor. Do you say 'poor Anne-Marie'? Or not? Probably not. The injured are 'poor'. Only they. Or the dead. 'A gaggle of spinsters,' you joked, bravely facing your condition head on, 'the unwise virgins, you might call us, are hardly the people to bring up a boy. *You* . . .'

I?

More Kir. I sent you an expensive cashmere sweater and thanked you for the wine. Not wishing to feel obligated.

'I think of him,' your letter had astonishingly gone on to say, 'as more your son than Lucette's. She was so briefly married, after all. Poor Gérard . . .'

'Poor' again. Think of Gérard so as not to think of Sam! Gérard married my sister, Lucette – the only one of you all who managed to have a date or get a man. Well, how could you, living up the mountains where the few middle-class males around were intent on showing the place a clean pair of heels as soon as they could pass their Bac? Lucette snatched Gérard during a six-week trip to Pau where she was taking the waters with an invalid aunt. She didn't do too badly, considering. He was reasonable-looking, a lawyer, and the fact that he would slip down a crevasse in our mountains could neither be foreseen nor held against him. I remember her triumph and the jealousy of everyone else, including our brother, Jacques, who had failed his exams that summer and thought he was stuck on the farm for life. As it happened, the Algerian war broke out and he joined the paratroopers. Another mourning card.

'I feel,' you write, 'that our family has a jinx on its men.'

Have I jinxed Sam? No, he was mad before. But maybe our two jinxes flew together like magnets. Clang! What's 'mad'?

Weren't the best people 'mad', Kiki? All the risking saints and poets? Not that I want to risk. Only to be happy. Though trying too hard for that may be risky too? Like grabbing some frail, untenable flower – say a water-lily – in one's fist. Lethal. Funny: promises frighten me. I think it's because our childhood was all promise. At least that's how I remember it. I wonder: are our memories the same? Mine are parrot-bright with the sun blazing off the Alps at the end of our orchard, fruit clotting, fireflies swooping, curtains of honey being shaken from its wax in our cellars and, 'for the orphans', endless name-day and birthday parties. We were twice orphaned. First your mother died, then mine: Papa's second wife. The aunts couldn't make it up to us enough. Couldn't cosset us enough. And to me all those parties seemed an endlessly renewed celebration of some happiness to come: promises. Even the summer storms on the Alps, the red and green lightning flashes on the white peaks – can you still see them from the dining-room window? – like the flames on our birthday candles, *had* to be heralding something marvellous. Do you remember that we felt that? And how when we were getting a little older and had begun to see that all the rituals ever led up to was indigestion and a stack of smeary washing-up, one or other of us would have hysterics, throw a tantrum, weep, scream or insult the aunts? From the time I was twelve and the rest of you were in your late teens or early twenties, all the birthdays ended like that. It was expected: a kind of release. When one of us threw down her hand at bridge or her chair to rush weeping from the room, the rest felt spared. Until the next time when we would start hoping all over again. I wonder: do you remember it all differently? You may. You were hunchbacked and didn't expect to leave. When the others stopped hoping, you may have felt pleased. When *I* left you didn't mind. I was the youngest and you had plenty of company without me. Besides, it was recognized that Anne-Marie was 'flighty' and the flighty take flight. Now, oddly, you are turning your attention to me again. Old devious Kiki, leaning back on your hump in our parents' old bed and scheming away to get me to take Jean-Luc. I know why of course. Money. I got my mother's. She was much richer than yours was and when my brother, Jacques, died all her money came to me. You got the house and land. They were Papa's. But you have no cash. If I would take Jean-Luc off your hands it would help. So you are at work on me, trying to teleguide me through some layer of my own forgetfulness. I feel you tuning subliminal messages to me. Maybe that's what's bringing me back to you when maybe I should have gone looking for Sam? Mad Sam. Poor, sweet Sam.

It's not because I'm afraid of him that I didn't go to him when I left Dirk and Rosemary's. I mean I was that too but the disturbing, frightening thing was that I hadn't noticed his madness! In eight months. I kept wondering about those months as I sat in Dirk and Rosemary's drawing-room. I kept remembering jokes which had perhaps not been jokes at all but sheer lunacy: moans perhaps, sick grunts with no meaning except the purely arbitrary ones supplied by me. Where had Sam's mind been? How much was intact? When had he been sane? When not? Was sleeping with him like sleeping with a sexy Great Dane who happened to be attached to a human mistress? An unadulterated, mindless fuck? Bestiality? Oh God, I muttered and was reminded of one of Sam's jokes which was calling God and his heavenly brains' trust 'Joe & Co.' (From Jove? Jahve?)

'Joe and Co. are having themselves a ball,' he'd say when things went wrong. He imagined them up there as malign and only minimally powerful. Impish, they enjoyed sending nasty surprises of a minor sort. Right now they certainly were having themselves a ball.

'Go damn yourselves, Joe and Co.!' I screamed.

Rosemary came in. 'Something wrong?'

'No.'

She went back to the kitchen.

Kiki, I wonder about my own sanity.

You see everything that Sam said made sense to me. Sound sense, even a sort of super-sense. Even all that stuff about Joe & Co. was a sign that Sam, poor, bright, suffering Sam, *knew* – must have – about the lousy hand he'd been dealt. He knew he was a nut – which makes him that much the less of one, doesn't it? I mean he was lucid and sadly generous – he warned me, after all, though he was in love with me. I'm pretty sure of that. And all's fair when you're in love. Yet he *did* give me a fair chance to back out. As much as he dared. As much as a sane man in love would.

But why did he love me? Did he recognize some congenial folly in me?

I have known freaks before. I told you. I'm not going to go into that. Only far enough to say that I seem to attract them and now wonder why. Like calling to like?

Or *they* attract *me*? Maybe. The thing is I hate the social game, the mean commerce of it, and when I see a man refuse to play I'm attracted. Meaning? Oh nothing subtle. Just the old, sleazy double-thinks, the mild moral sag you meet every day in successful men and which successful men don't a bit mind revealing to women like me. They take off their attitudes as they might their clothes and don't suppose we'll notice contradictions. We do though. They're the very things to which we're alert. When you take your values from your men, as women do – as *I* find myself doing simply because my dealings with the world, society or what-have-you are usually *through* a man – then you'd like to think they're decent values and when they're not you notice. It's not, for God's sake, that I'm a prig – that would be a laugh, wouldn't it? – but, well, I do object to phoniness doing a smelly striptease under my nose and then asking me to admire its imperial vestments. But Sam, you see, was different. Unphony. Honest. Mad.

Oh I don't know. His jokes, now that I think back, weren't all that funny. He was usually smashed or stoned when he clowned. I suppose he was a bit childish. Once, for instance, he ordered ket-chup in a very chichi inn outside Paris: the sort of place that has bits of saddlery on the wall and a rosette in the Michelin Guide. They'd never heard of ketchup.

'I want some,' Sam insisted. 'In a bottle. *Appellation controlée.*' Then he snatched up a carving knife and threatened the waiter. 'Ketchup,' he told him, 'is part of my cultural heritage. Do you despise it?'

The waiter said he didn't.

Then Sam charged into the kitchen to interrogate the chef. I stayed where I was until the manageress begged me to intervene. If Sam hadn't looked so strong they would have thrown him out. But he did. The inn was in the country. No time to call the police. When I reached the kitchen, Sam was prodding the chef in the belly with the point of his knife. 'Where do you think they get the blood for Spaghetti Westerns?' he was asking him. 'Not *here*.' Another prod. 'Ketchup . . .'

77

Now I know the chef was right to be afraid and the thing was less funny than I thought. Oh Kiki, maybe you're right and I never did grow up!

'After all,' said Rosemary coming in to poke up the fire and justify herself. 'You are older than Sam, Anne-Marie!' She went off.

Meaning? That I was over-the-hill. Should be pleased with what I could get! A fine stud like Sam. What's a bit of wife-battery in a deal like that? Or did she just mean 'old enough to know better'? Probably.

'Where's Sam?' I asked when we were at table.

'At his mother's,' Dirk told me. 'You'll have to hide,' he advised. 'He's dangerous.'

'He attacked her once,' Rosemary told me. 'His mother. With a knife. You can't blame her for not telling you.'

She was spooning *cassoulet* into our plates and looking pleased, as conventional women often do when they get a thrill at second hand. 'I really admire Marsha,' she said excitedly. 'She's been through it with Sam.'

Oh God, I thought, don't let her tell me more. Don't let her. But already she was swallowing down her *cassoulet* and wiping her mouth, all agog. She opened it. 'He . . .' she began.

'He's been through her,' I said to shut her up. I stared angrily at her. She was fatly pregnant and smug. 'The uterus,' I went on fast and loudly, 'forms a creature on the model of the object loved by the mother. This opinion was put forward by the British biologist, Harvey, some time in the sixteen-fifties. Do you suppose Sam's mother loved a circus-freak? Or a murderer or butcher perhaps?' I waved my glass, spilling some reddish drops on the cloth. I rubbed salt into them conscientiously. 'She may always have longed to be attacked with a knife, you see?'

Dirk and Rosemary looked as though they'd eaten something bad.

'I'm in love with Sam,' I began to cry.

Dirk left the table. Rosemary put the *cassoulet* back on the stove.

She put a hand on my arm. Rosemary's not a toucher. She was making an effort. 'Sam's a friend of ours, Anne-Marie,' she said gently. 'We like him. We have for years. He's O K most of the time.'

'Yes. I'm sorry. It's not you,' I accused myself. 'It's me.' I was crying into my wine. I had poured more into my glass and was now drinking a ghastly mixture of Kir, Côtes du Rhône and tears.

'Look,' said Rosemary, 'you'd better go to bed.'

She took the glass from me and led me to a small bedroom, pulled off my shoes and left me lying on a revolving bed. I suppose she went back down to call Dirk to eat the rest of his *cassoulet*.

I tried to remember what I'd said and she'd said before we had begun to argue, but I couldn't. I knew I'd mentioned you and that she'd been relieved to find I had somewhere to go.

'A trip to the country,' she said approvingly, 'would be just the thing. You can't go back to Sam's place.'

Oh Kiki!

'Now,' you wrote, 'that you're going to have a home again!'

You've put the evil eye on me.

Sam, Sam, Sam, Sam!

The trouble is most men don't appeal to me at all. I don't *see* them! When I find one who does I think: Maybe he's the last!

I'm drinking again. The train funnels down the diagonal from Paris to Chambéry, and as it does I find myself taking more and more little swigs. Hine. I feel its glow in my throat, chest and deep in my old, cold, ardent, widowed belly. Inner caresses, consolings, comforts. Kiki, I wish you drank. I often think of the thinness of your life and wonder do people whose pleasures are few get more and extra enjoyment from them? An intenser, richer yield? Unlikely. Inequality reigns here too.

I try to remember what pleasures you have enjoyed since growing up. Do you still go to Chambéry to eat the cakes for which it is famous? reminding yourself that this, at least, is, though a minor pleasure, the very best of its kind?

'I know,' says your fingered and furry letter, 'you have had abortions. Whatever you thought your reasons were, I feel one contributing cause was the fact that we made you into a baby for life. And how can a baby have a baby? Mind you, to have one might be the best thing for you. If you were to take Jean-Luc . . .'

'You have,' you write, 'had abortions . . .'

Have you an image to put with that firmly used word? I have.

I asked Sam would he like us to have a baby.

'Ten,' he said, 'or five. I'm in favour of the decimal system. So French! Or point one of one.'

'Shut up!' I said. 'I've seen a fractured baby. Well: foetus.'

'How much of it?'

'Never mind.'

'Which parts?'

'No!'

'I'm interested.'

'For Christ's sake, Sam!'

'I'm only talking. You did it.'

'You have,' I conceded, 'a point.'

'Decimal point.'

'You're sick.'

And of course he was. *Merde!* Bugger Joe & Co.! I took several valium, not counting the number. And got to sleep.

I dreamed of an abortionist I used to know and visited twice as a client. He kept embryos in glass bottles in his garden as people keep pottery elves. It was an isolated garden and he kept some live iguanas there too in a kind of chicken run. Unlike you, Kiki, who deal with things fearlessly in the abstract, he liked to stare head-on at what he was doing. Perhaps that was where he put his pride.

'Don't you know,' you said, turning up suddenly in my dream, 'that you're Jean-Luc's mother? You had a premature baby when you were sixteen and we never told you. It was smaller than these pottery elves. We were able to make you believe you had been bedridden for months with TB, then deliver you under an anaesthetic and pretend the baby was Lucette's. *She* had a husband, you see. Now if you were to take charge . . .'

'Who's the father then?'

'Ah,' you said, 'a touch of incest. Men,' you said, 'are scarce around our house. Read the bible and you'll see how they managed. It was a way of keeping patrimonies intact. Read about Lot's daughters.'

'You're mad,' I shrieked.

'It means,' you said, 'that you owe us the money you took out of the family.'

'Mad!'

'Not me,' you said. 'You're the one. Disgraced the family. You gave birth to an iguana.'

'Are you all right?'

Someone was rattling my bedroom door. Dirk, my host. I'd locked it.

'Yes,' I shouted, 'a nightmare. Sorry.'

'For God's sake,' he said, 'do you always scream like that?'

He stumped off, muttering. I took some more valium.

At breakfast he said, 'Look, I'm sorry, Anne-Marie, but Rosemary needs her sleep. She's pregnant, you know. I'm afraid *you're* in need of care. You look as though you might be having a breakdown. Haven't you got any family you can go to? Anyway you can't stay here. Sam might come looking for you.'

Later, when we were in his car driving to Paris, he asked me where I wanted to go.

I said I might go and see Marsha.

For minutes Dirk seemed to concentrate on his driving. Then: 'Look,' he said, 'I think I'd better warn you. Marsha's a bit of a bitch. She wants to get remarried, you see, and it would facilitate this if Sam were in good hands: yours. To put it brutally, she's looking for an unpaid nurse. Don't believe what she tells you. Sam's incurable. Schizoid. He can be sound as a bell for months but he always reverts. It can happen any time. I *know* this. I'm sorry, Anne-Marie,' he said. 'You've got to face it.'

'Yes.'

'Where?' he asked when we reached the city.

'My things are in Sam's flat.'

'I'll get them. You wait,' he said. He parked the car two streets away from the apartment building and took my keys. 'Read the paper,' he advised. 'I'll be as quick as I can. If I overlook some stuff, Marsha can send it on later. When you have an address.'

'Thanks.'

He was back in less than half an hour with my cases. 'No sign of Sam,' he said as he put them in the boot. 'I packed everything feminine-looking,' he explained. 'Not very tidily, I'm afraid.'

'Thanks,' I said again.

'Where now?'

'Take me to the Gare de Lyon.' I knew he wanted to be rid of me. 'I have relatives in Savoy,' I reassured him.

'Well,' he said when he dropped me off, 'if there's anything you want . . . you know.' Vaguely and looking relieved.

'That's OK.'

When he left I found a phone and rang Marsha. I wasn't sure what I was going to say but she *was* responsible for what had happened.

'Marsha, this is Anne-Marie. Do you know what happened yesterday?'

I was still hoping she'd have some explanation or antidote. 'Do you?' I asked.

Her voice rushed down the wire and I knew it was all no good. She was crying and on the booze. 'I haven't been fair to you,' she was sobbing.

'Is he curable?'

'Can you come over? Where are you, Anne-Marie?'

'Is he?'

'What, dear?'

'Curable?'

More sobs. She kept saying my name. 'Listen,' she said, 'there was a terrible scene here last night and the police came. He attacked one of them. They took him away. I don't know *where*. I have a lawyer trying to find out . . . listen, Anne-Marie, we must meet. Can't you come now?'

'You didn't answer my question.'

'I'm a mother,' Marsha sobbed. 'A mother,' she repeated. It sounded like the responses to a litany of reproach. But I hadn't reproached her. 'Can't you understand?' she asked.

'Yes,' I said. 'I can. I do.' I put down the phone.

I went to the station buffet and had a cognac.

'Marsha,' Dirk had warned me, 'is as tough as old nails. Very calculating.'

I had a second cognac. Was Sam Sam, I wondered? Did the man I thought I was in love with exist and what did I owe him? I mean if he's not responsible for himself, how can I be? I've had my heart smashed up before, Kiki, like a pulverized elbow. I've found people change in my grasp like the Old Man of the Sea. I haven't the strength to go through that again. I put the glass on the counter, went to the ticket office and bought a single for Chambéry.

A one-way single to solitude. Oh Jesus! Oh Joe!

Time out for a drink. Finished the Hine. Last lovely drops still hot on my mouth. Dijon out there. Closer now to you than to Sam, Kiki. No!

Kiki, I'm not coming back. I know. I know what you'd say but you're not going to get a chance. Besides: you don't even know I'd set out, do you? Glad I never rang now. Pre-ordained: Joe & Co. at their more short-term benevolent. Always means they've something bloody up their drifty sleeve. Never mind. Defy the bastards! I'm going back.

I'm not normal. O K? I never thought I was. I was just too belly-crawlingly humble: persuading myself that the majority, because a majority, must be right. You belong to it, Kiki, and Jean-Louis and Rosemary and Dirk and Marsha and all the mothers and parents of all the lovers and the lovers when they stop loving and the mad when they're sane. Joe & Co. I'm not sure of. I think they're schizoid. But Sam and I are nuts and I'm the better nut because I choose nuttiness. I'll stand by mad Sam.

My own monster.

Look: you don't need me and neither does Jean-Luc. My bit of money would only buy you a dose of smothering gentility. That's all. *We* can't talk, Kiki. I've been trying to talk to you all the way from bloody Paris, all across this uptight, sour, canny, old, tired, knowing, horrible hexagon of a country where everything you can say's been said and the best things, down to the cheese and wine, are fermentings of crushed other things. I'm going off to be mad. I know it's a bit negative, a bit limited but, Kiki, I'm only me. I'd be no good looking after you – we'd brain each other – or bringing meals-on-wheels to the aged. I'm good for Sam though and he's sometimes good for me and . . . oh fuck, why try to talk?

Which brings me to a final point you might just grasp. I might xerox it on three hundred and sixty-five scraps of paper and send you one daily and then one chance day it just might – might – connect. It's this: I don't live to fuck, Kiki. I fuck to live. It's an aid, a prop. Listen: I'm not being outrageous for kicks, just trying to tell you that I'm thirty-five years old and look more. They were packed years. I'm not the girl you disapproved of at seventeen with a somewhat scuffed-up face. I'm a different person. That girl ignored your advice. She took the risks you rightly warned her against. She got burned. Right? You were right then but – watch it, Kiki, here's the surprise: that makes you wrong now. Because people who've stayed carefully out of the fire and people who've been through it are not the same. They're a different race and Sam's my race and you're not. So you can't advise me and I can't talk to you and I'm getting off this train at the next stop and getting the next one back to the *ville lumière* where I shall flame like a salamander until I go up in smoke.

And I wish to Joe & Co. I had some more lovely Hine, because I bloody need it. Wonder will the buffet be open at the next station?

Because don't think I think it's going to be easy. I'm terrified.

Mad Marga

'Lady to see you. A Miss . . .' The porter fumbled the name: 'Baby-blacker? Something like that. She's at the gate lodge. They rang through.'

'Now?' queried James. It was ten p.m.

'She rang,' the porter said vaguely, 'last night, was it? I told her you'd be working late this evening. I meant to mention her to you, but it slipped my mind.'

'What does she want?'

The man shrugged or maybe suffered a tremor. He had some sort of palsy. 'She's American,' he offered.

It was the policy of the Blumfontein Art Institute to give low-level jobs to men who might have had trouble getting them anywhere else. James, the director, had no say in the matter.

'It's a condition of Mr Blumfontein's will,' the chief trustee had told him. 'Philanthropy. Shouldn't affect your end of things since it only applies to unskilled personnel.'

'What if one of your charity cases goes berserk and attacks the paintings?' James had asked.

The trustee had a smile for this. 'We're businessmen, James. You may rely on us to protect the Institute's property.' He had gone on to explain about burglar alarms.

James felt put in his place and that probably his place, in the mind of the chief trustee, would not be far from that of the disabled porter. The trustee had been an associate of the Institute's founder – a tough, not to say brutal, South African who had made his money in unsavoury ways. When the Institute first opened, there had been some picketing and articles in the radical press. James, who had accepted the directorship about then, was not, he told

85

friends, condoning Blumfontein's crimes, just glad that good should come of them. Anyway, wasn't there a nice symmetry to this buccaneer's leaving loot for fifteenth-century Italian art, just as fifteenth-century usurers used to leave theirs to the church?

'Am I to send her away, then?' The porter spoke like a man used to being in the wrong. 'She said she was a friend of yours.'

'What was the name again?'

'Foreign name. Bavylacca?' The man's arms opened as though to embrace a box.

Suddenly James knew who it was. 'A stout lady?'

'That's right.'

Marga Bevilacqua! James hadn't seen her for – oh, a dozen years. How like her not to write and turn up at such an hour. No nous, no grace: the old Marga. At the same time, a warm feeling bubbled up in him.

The porter's gesture reminded him of his own first impression of her: girth. She was calling herself Peg then, and the name went badly with her Italian surname. 'A square peg,' had been James's thought, 'jiggling round a hole!' The erotic implication was too cruel for laughter, and because he couldn't dispose of her that way he'd given her a second glance. What he saw was a plain, passionate girl who had begun to fear that she was unfitted for the only destiny she could imagine for herself – matrimony. Poor Square Peg! He had advised her to call herself Marga.

'All right,' he told the porter. 'Phone through that they can let her come.'

James had rescued her – this became a shared joke – from the bullying K K K dream of Küche, Kinder, Kirche: a good act, since she could never have achieved it. Maybe things would have been different if she had married at eighteen? By the time he met her she had become a yearner with an appetite so keen that its scope was metaphysical. James was fascinated and eager to steer this force into appropriate channels. To be fair to himself, his main motive had been kindness. But in a way he couldn't put his finger on, he had, for a time, become dependent on Marga. Odd. James laughed at the oddness of it.

Marga would be on her way up the long avenue. Should he have sent a car? Surely she would have one? He had no idea what she did for a living. When they'd met she'd been a typist and he an art historian employed by an American foundation. Their salaries were princely by London standards, and hers went almost entirely on her back. She spent nothing on food, eating perhaps one yogurt for lunch in the subsidized canteen. She was involved in an all out struggle with her recalcitrant flesh.

'Like an old-time saint,' James had teased. His field was the quattrocento, and extremes of asceticism and carnality excited him. Both met in Marga, whose preoccupation with her anatomy was stern. Once or twice she came to work unmade-up, and he remembered marvelling how, as the day wore on, her wistful travesty of a *Vogue*-ish ideal was assembled step by step. Identities fractured before his eyes: the one she wanted, the one doing the wanting, and – touching as a child's drawing – the bright, crude mask with which she ended up. By noon, with her eyelashes on, she was starting to remind him of a cow called Maybelle who had promoted processed cheese in the ads of his boyhood. These had appeared in American magazines which reached England at a time when the things they promoted were unavailable, making post-war schoolboys like James salivate over such pictured marvels as pineapple, Hershey bars, and something golden, phallic, and unknown called corn on the cob. When an American soldier gave James an actual Hershey bar, the discovery that it was less good than ordinary English chocolate shattered a sustaining faith.

Peg subscribed to the very magazines which had dazzled him. He saw them furled in the bucket bags she slung about her. These made her look even more like Maybelle and Gladys. There had been a whole family of those cows, he remembered now, all chewing cheese, a sort of auto-destructive cycle – surely eating the product of your udder was next thing to eating yourself? Peg's udders jutted like dispensing-machine spouts. She came from a place in Iowa called Council Bluffs and would never have left it if her fluent Italian, learned from immigrant parents, had not got her a job in this Renaissance institute where she served sulkily, like a slave ravished on the eve of her nuptials and sold into bondage. Longing for domesticity, she had no career ambitions at all. She never looked at the paintings or bothered to attend lectures on art. Yet to James she seemed an embodiment of the artistic impulse: working against the grain of her nature, striving, pursuing a dream. When she told him she only stayed here because she had got used to the money, he could not believe this, and when one of the other American employees told him she thought Peg an ordinary small-town girl, he was astonished.

'Surely not?'

'I promise you,' said the girl. 'Peg's maybe not too pretty, but she wants what girls from those places want: a man, a house, babies.' The girl laughed to deprecate disloyalty and distinguish herself from Peg, who was only a typist – whereas she, the speaker, having a glorious degree from Vassar College, wore flat shoes, no lipstick, and didn't have to try. The implication was that she could get these same goodies with one hand tied behind her.

'Oh,' said James. 'It's like dreaming about unobtainable Hershey bars.' He saw that this girl, whose mind had been alerted to Freudian symbols at Vassar, supposed he was being smutty. Like Peg, she was programmed, but as her programme was working for her she was unlikely to see its limitations.

Peg was acutely aware of hers. She sloshed paint across her face in a superstitious rather than a hopeful spirit. Her hair had recently been dyed pink and her clothes bought rather as fetishistic symbols than with an eye to suitability. Distrust in her system was blatant. 'All things betray thee, who betrayest Me,' quoted James in his own mind, and was reminded of paintings of the young Saint Francis throwing off the raiment of his wastrel days. Peg's passion must be working towards its peak and turning-point. He felt an urge to hasten it along and asked whether she had ever considered cutting her hair short. Something severe.

'It would suit you. Play up the strength of your face.'

Attention thrilled her – she got so little. Yet – he saw doubt move across her face – might his be the wrong sort? She knew James had taste. Everyone said so. They also said that he had special preferences, and mightn't the ones undermine the other? Was he trying to make her mannish? Well, thought James, we'll just have to get past that one, won't we?

It must have been about then that he introduced her to the boy he was living with. Gio, an apprentice waiter in a Soho restaurant, looked anything but mannish. He had long Bernini curls. They suited *him*; a Bernini boy all over. Beautiful and self-regarding, he might have been made of bronze or, no – some more ductile, re-usable material like wax. This was unkind. Gio was sharp, in a ferret-like way, but dealt fairly with James. It was just that he lacked a dimension: sensibility? soul? Some northern requirement. The lack left gaps in James's emotional life and James used Marga's friendship to fill them in.

That autumn, on a trip to Florence – it was a treat for Gio, whose family lived there – James lay on the rim of a Giambologna fountain staring up Neptune's thigh at soul-made-stone: tensile and denying its own essence, tremulous with the life it didn't have. Soul, he decided, was dissatisfaction. It was revolt against the im-perfections which hem us in and figure death. Gio, it was clear, didn't have it. Peg did. Frustration had bred it in her. She knew that longing which, missing its object, was apt, in earlier ages, to leap up and fasten on God. On what should it fasten now?

Across from James, on the stage set of the Loggia dei Lanzi, a bronze Judith held up Holofernes' dripping, severed head. Sabine women in greyed marble were ravished as Peg surely dreamed of being ravished: held aloft in palpitating curves of passive grace. Hold *her* that way and she'd look like a removalman's burden: an upside-down armchair or a toppled Pegasus. Oh dear, another Peg joke.

Yet back in London she became his private Pegasus, lifting him up, providing respites from the quarrelsome carnality of his life with Gio. Unable to free himself from his lower nature, he launched a campaign against hers.

'You've got to be freed from thinginess, Marga,' he instructed.

Her room, which she now let him visit, proved to be a temple to the flesh, a prop-shop filled with gadgets for curling, massaging, slimming, opening pores, humidifying, and procuring a winter tan. He recognized these as the instruments of despair, something like the emblems displayed in the portraits of the saints and martyrs of his period. She was irredeemably ugly. But what did that matter, he thought. If only she could see that it didn't matter at all.

Came the spring of 1968, and anti-consumerism was in full spate on the walls of Paris where James, back from another trip to

Florence, stopped off with Gio. He noted a number of slogans which Peg/Marga ought, he told her, to take to heart. She should, he exhorted, live up to the battling abbess's face, which was hers now that she had shed her frizz of hair. He lent her books, extolled collective over individual passion, and took her to demos in Trafalgar Square. Demands for gay, minority, and women's rights were riding a tide of festive energy and goodwill.

Society, James wrote on Marga's bathroom mirror, *is a carnivorous flower*.

Shriek, he advised. *Yell.*

Advertising has you in thrall.

Some of the Paris slogans didn't translate well. *Man screws objects*, he tried, then *Objects screw men.*

French was a better language for this sort of thing, he assured her. Italian too. Maybe she should spend her summer vacation in her parents' old country instead of visiting them in Council Bluffs? Things were brewing in Italy, he told her. Energy was like ozone in its air. Last month in Florence, coming from a church full of Masaccio frescoes, he had stepped into a crowd of demonstrators. In the stony light, their faces resembled the ones he had just been admiring: dour, shrewd Tuscan faces, one or two with jaws like hers. A man had called James *compagno*.

'If you get politicized,' he told her, 'you'll never be alone.'

'Right now, you're stuck,' he accused her, 'stuck in consumerism like a fly in jam.' Flipping derisively through one of her glossy magazines, he mocked its advice on how to hook your man, how to become Mrs X or Mrs Y. 'You,' instructed James, 'should have the nerve to just be you.' He was gratified by the way she blossomed under his attention.

He must have seen her on less emphatic occasions. He forgot. Shortly after that conversation, he left his job, having been appointed to look after the art collection of a small New England college. When he returned to England, Marga had left it. Perhaps they had crossed in mid-Atlantic, square-dancing between continents? He heard that she had tried life in Council Bluffs for a while, hoping perhaps to settle with some ageing boy-next-door? Then he ran into the Vassar girl at a party and heard some garbled gossip.

'Did you hear that Peg joined the Weathermen, or was it the

PLO?' The girl, now a woman, had changed identities in that effortless way some Americans could. Painted and maternity gowned, she alighted beside him between the coffee and liqueurs. '*You've* got a lot to answer for,' she chid him brightly. Peg, it seemed, had been involved in some scandal – a kidnapping or perhaps only a sit-in. Anyway, her name had got into the papers: Marga Bevilacqua. 'That was your idea, wasn't it? Such an operatic name!' reproached the ex-Vassarite. 'It seems to have gone to her head. What did a girl like that have to be dissatisfied about? She had a good job. Her father was only a truck driver, you know. And where did all that protest get anyone in the end?' She'd heard rumours that Peg had had to go underground, but maybe they weren't true? She hoped not. In America, she told James, change and social mobility came to those who waited. No need for impatience. An Englishman mightn't be aware of that. 'Of course Peg,' she added absolvingly, 'was never well balanced.'

'Miss Bevilacqua,' announced the porter with practised accuracy. Marga must have won his heart.

'Marga!'

'Jim!'

They kissed, then held each other at arm's length.

'You've changed,' she yelped.

'For the worse?' James was vain. Then he realized that she had deflected his scrutiny of her. Clever old Marga! '*You've* regressed,' he noted with surprise. Her head was once more aureoled with yellow frizz.

'A wig!' She pulled it off. 'I'm in my bourgeois gear. Your porter wouldn't have let in a weirdo, would he? By the way, I've got a friend downstairs.'

'The porter shouldn't have let him in,' James remarked. 'Shall we have him brought up?'

'Her. Later, perhaps, I have a way with porters. Fortunately. Getting in here was like crashing a party in the Kremlin.'

'Well, you could have written. What are you doing in these parts?'

'What are *you*?' Firm scrutiny. She began to circulate around James's study, staring at walls and furniture. Dumpy as ever, she was tied like a flour sack into an old camel coat. Her bourgeois gear? The hair she had uncovered was tufty, grey and short. She had a large shoulder bag, and her legs were thrust into stumpy brogues.

'I heard you became a revolutionary,' he said, uncertain whether to tease.

'Your lot don't think much of us here,' he observed to her back. She was examining the place like a surveyor. 'We were picketed,' he admitted, wanting Marga to agree that he'd been right to take this job and hadn't succumbed to what they used to call the three middles: middle age, middle class, and middle of the road. He couldn't put his case though, until she turned around. You had to see a person's expression, try to make them smile.

'Is that a cupboard?' She tapped a door with her knuckles. 'Or does it lead somewhere?'

'It's a false door,' he told her. 'It goes with the panelling. Bog oak and holly. We had it brought from a house in Buckinghamshire. Marga, darling, you're making me babble! I wish you'd sit down. Anyone would think you were casing the joint for a burglary.'

She sat. 'You're not far out.'

'Were you really an activist?' he asked. 'That female – the one with buck teeth who shared an office with you – told me you were. She couldn't remember any details.'

Marga shrugged.

How old she's got, he thought. She was leaning back, eyes closed the way you saw overworked people do on late-night buses. Hadn't the porter said something about her working late? At what? She didn't look like a secretary. She looked like an Oxfam lady who wore the best of the charity clothes herself.

She probably needed the catnap she was taking, yet James couldn't resist trying to rouse her. Like a child throwing a nut at a somnolent zoo animal, he asked whether he had been responsible for politicizing her.

She answered without opening her eyes, 'Oh you needn't bear that guilt. If it hadn't been your advice I took, it might have been my horoscope's. No' – James had made hurt sounds – 'I'm not forgetting your kindness.' She opened her eyes and he remembered that they were her one good feature. Deep blue and large, they looked as though they belonged to someone else. 'You gave me the first push,' she told him. 'You felt I wasn't fit for ordinary living, so I'd better be extraordinary. You thought I *could* be. You were wrong, but that's another matter.'

Again her lids drooped, shutting in that bright, vivacious blue. James, filtering jocularity into his tone, said he'd heard rumours about her having been involved in some violence. The remark about his thinking her unfit for ordinary living embarrassed him. Yet he'd been fond of her. He still felt a connection with her, as though she had been his child or mother or some aspect of himself which had fallen on the thorns of life while he, home and dry, had been able to go on enjoying his profession. She looked derelict, sitting in that Gothic chair.

'*We* never chose violence,' she said firmly. What did she mean by 'we'? Who were 'we'?

'You mean,' he remembered the current rhetoric, 'that it was part of the system?'

'What was?'

'Violence.'

She gave a half-snore. Was she going to fall asleep?

Talk! he wanted to shout. You came here to make contact, I presume? Ask me about Gio. No don't. Gio was now the father of four and the sweaty part-owner of a restaurant in Bagno a Ripoli. How much of whose money went into all that chrome and neon, James had wondered, foolishly visiting the place last summer.

'You respond to institutionalized violence,' he reminded her, 'with revolutionary violence. Isn't that the argument?' Words rolled off his tongue. Irony seemed to coat them. 'You choose the lesser evil in an attempt to eliminate the greater one.' It sounded like a send-up. It was his fluency. His accent perhaps? That sort of speech had to be made as if you were dragging thought from some painful depth of your soul. A third-world person could deliver it best, or dotty old Marga, but the poor cow seemed to be asleep. Frightening to remember that she was younger than he. Two years younger. God!

'James!' She had roused herself and was leaning forward. 'Is there a back way out of this room?'

'No. Why do you ask?' He waited, then launched his joke: 'You're not on the run, I hope?'

'Listen.' She had lowered her voice. 'I'm sorry to spring this on you, but I couldn't have written or anything because you might have told the police.'

Oh God! Trouble. What kind? The grey-faced woman, Marga, was sweating that peculiar smelly sweat which meant fear. James had encountered it in Italy. Once he had agreed to be the outside examiner in an exam for tourist guides and been confronted with what the comfortable jokingly call 'the great unwashed'. Peasant boys from farms, girls with only this single hope of getting out of husbandless small towns had competed for a very few places and sweated sour terror across the examiner's table at James, It had befuddled him then. It was doing so now.

'Marga, you know I'll . . . are you really in trouble?'

She had opened her handbag and was taking out a gun. It was a nasty-looking thing with a snout. James knew from cinema experience that the snout was a silencer.

She laid it on his desk. 'Take it. The woman downstairs is armed too: Annie. They don't trust me. We were sent to destroy your Pieros. They picked me because they know I used to know you. I couldn't say "no".'

The four pictures by Piero della Francesca were the collection's pride and its core. James felt seized by a curious rigidity. His brain had not adjusted to the situation.

'Hear me out,' said Marga, and added that she had never for one moment intended going through with the plan. 'It's the kind of dumb gesture *they* go in for. They – the people who set this up – claim to be anti-materialistic, but you become the thing you fight: object-obsessed . . .' James's brain seemed to divide. Half of it monitored her babble about the people who had her in their control. The other part of his brain was passive, overrun by emotion. 'I'm wanted in Italy,' he heard Marga say. 'If they denounce me, or if the cops here get me, I could be extradited.'

'What room is this woman in?' asked James's alert self. 'How many of you are there?' The Pieros, he was thinking – oh God, the Pieros. Their luminosity became fractured inside his head. The two sides of his mind clashed like cymbals.

'There's a car outside the gate, but there are only us in the house. Annie has a machine gun in her briefcase. It doesn't take her thirty seconds to assemble it. She's in the hall where the fountain is. These people think they're God . . .'

She went on speaking, saying other things, telling who the groups were. There were several groups, he gathered. They lent each other people. She had been lent. International cooperation within the framework of . . . Meanwhile he was seeing the woman down in the hall, waiting. Would she get impatient? There were two fourteenth-century *predelle* right there for her to destroy. His heart raced. The precarious quality of beauty had always pained him, and here was brutal justification for his fear. Rubbish. No. She'd come for the Pieros. She'd have more patience, more control than he. How long *had* Marga been here? The keys to the Piero room were in his pocket. The women must have known that. Damage to the *predelle* – anonymous, much less newsworthy – would be a waste of their expedition. She won't do it. James. Keep *calm*.

'You knew I had the keys?' But he'd guessed the answer before she told him: the porter. His foot edged toward the burglar alarm button in the floor. No. *Wait*. He was sweating now. Marga had begun pulling on her doll-like wig. He let her talk. Coldly he waited for useful facts, his foot poised near the alarm button.

She was afraid of extradition, she said, pulling wisps of frizz over the hairline. If the Italians got her they'd lock her up and throw away the key. She'd been framed by her fellow militants. 'That's policy. You get someone implicated in a crime, then they can't get away from you.' Fiddling with the bangs of her Mrs Middle-America wig, Marga claimed that she only wanted to be ordinary, but now they wouldn't let her. She had been with a feminist group who had shot a gynaecologist in the legs. 'It was in Rome. Maybe you heard of the case? He used to charge extortionate fees to perform abortions on poor women, so it was decided that he should be made to see what it was like to be imprisoned in your body. They crippled him,' said Marga, but said that she had not known of the plan in advance. 'If I had, I might have gone along with it anyway. I don't know. It was like a punishment out of Dante. You remember *la legge del contrapasso*: you are punished even as you sinned?' James winced. Was he to be punished in the pictures, then? Marga had been press-ganged into joining further expeditions. In short, she had a record.

What about the woman downstairs, James asked. Wouldn't she be getting impatient?

'No,' said Marga. 'She'll give me time to chat with you. Then I'm to ask you if you'll show us both the Piero room. I'm to say she's an art student. If you refuse, I'm to bring you down at gunpoint with the keys.' However, she had a counterplan: James must agree to show the pictures. Annie would then be off-guard and, on the way to the Piero room, Marga and he would disarm her. Explaining her change of heart, Marga talked obsessively about herself. 'I,' she said, 'I.' Had she always been so self-centred, he wondered impatiently. Had *he* done this to her? Made a Frankenstein of her? He picked up the gun. She seemed not to notice. Had she invented the whole thing? Did the woman, Annie, exist? 'You're my link with the old life,' she was saying. '. . . A new start,' he heard, 'if you'll help me, James . . . help me to get away from them is all I ask.'

All, he thought, *all*? She must be insane. Maybe she always had been? If she was his creation, his Miss Frankenstein, then he had nothing to be proud of. Banalities poured from her. She unreeled the ragged frieze of her life while the four paintings dazzled his inner eye and he held her gun on his lap, trained on her but concealed by the desk. Why shouldn't she go to gaol, he thought. He had not the slightest pity for her.

'Things,' she said, 'Pictures are only things.'

He was aghast.

'*You* taught me,' she repeated, 'not to be fetishistic about material things. You said . . .' Laboriously she reported what she thought he had said. Had he? It sounded distorted in her mouth. 'But to destroy material things gives them importance,' she argued triumphantly, refuting her new mentors' arguments with what she took to be his. 'A form of idolatry,' she concluded. Christ, thought James, *Jesus Christ!* Art was like Christ's face glowing on Veronica's towel: the soul's graphic mark, the imprint of its passion, worth more than the botched lives of endless women like this.

Her face was rosy now, almost beautiful as she planned her treachery towards her confederate. James was to keep the gun in his pocket. 'She'll think it's your keys, see. I'll be behind and she'll think I've got you covered. Then you wave her ahead toward the Piero room. She'll expect you to do that for a lady. Then you stick the gun in her back.' Annie would then be handed over to the police while Marga herself was to be let quietly go. She'd be free of the law and of her terrorist companions. 'I'll just disappear,' she said, sounding for all the world like a woman in a soap opera of the sort she should have been watching at home in Iowa if she'd never left it. Then she was talking *about* Iowa, and how she would go back there where she had no record and used a different name.

It struck him that of course she had planned this – maybe even offered herself as go-between. She must have put the paintings at risk deliberately, in the hope that he would help her get away from her companion. How *could* the terrorists have known she knew James unless she had told them so herself? He had tried to groom her, to take away her ordinariness, and now he owed it to her to restore her to her habitat. She was actually saying something like this.

'No, but they used to call me your fag hag. Don't look hurt. Well, you wouldn't have wanted them thinking we were having an affair, right? You were so admired, and who was I in that outfit? Miss Nobody from the bottom of the barrel. I guess it amused you to pick me out to have lunches with: the prince and the goose girl. It amused you to surprise people. No, don't be offended, James. I was, I am grateful to you. Only, you see, I *am* a sort of goose girl. I really am. I want to go home to my own place.'

'Isn't that just fantasy? I thought you had tried living back in Council Bluffs?'

'It was too soon. Now I could. I was too radicalized then, and dressing the way you'd taught me, and I kept arguing with straight people. Now I'd love it. I just want to be where I know people, know the way they are, you know, and the rhymes the kids are skipping rope to, and where the teenagers go for their coke or dope or whatever. Feeling my way into them. Knowing their features from their parents.' She spoke rapidly, lyrically. Energy flowed back into her. She laughed. 'I could be the lady bank clerk in one of those dinky one-storey banks, or the saleslady at the health-food store looking out the window at green lawns and the white frame church. "Miss Bevilacqua?" people would say. "Sure, she's from here. Knew her dad. She went to Europe for a bit but she's home now . . ." '

James's foot pressed the button on the floor. He'd been meaning to do it, but when he did he surprised himself the way you can when you find you've turned off a radio programme without thinking: something cheap and invasive, maybe an ad or a tear-jerker that gets to you on levels of yourself which you don't like to acknowledge. Good, he thought, feeling back in control. The police station was less than a mile away. They'd be en route in no time, dousing their blue light on the last stretch and approaching the house with maximum discretion. The trustee had explained the drill. The woman, Annie, would not suspect a car or two coming quietly up the drive. Even if she did, she'd be disarmed before she knew it and Marga would, of course, have to be taken into custody. No deals. How could there be? Anyway, he doubted if she was quite sane. Years had passed since he'd known her. She'd probably taken drugs of various sorts, shot her brain to bits.

'Why don't you put on a light?'

'What?'

'It's dim here.' She indicated his green reading light, the discreet lamps. 'Or shall we go down now?'

'No, no,' he had to say. Then, 'Tell me more about Council Bluffs.'

She laughed, amused, unsuspecting. What a hopeless revolutionary she must have been. A hopeless human being. But were revolutionaries not mostly that? The rank and file of them anyway, the wretched background figures?

'Tell me,' he said, an image of the travelling police cars in his mind's eye. They'd be at the crossroads any minute. He must hold her here until they had dealt with the woman, Annie, and if there was no such person then no harm was done. He would have done the prudent thing. 'Is there a river there?' he asked.

'River?'

His mind swam. Why had he asked that? 'In your hometown?' Was he thinking of some song?

But it seemed that there was one, the Missouri River. There were oaks and sumac bushes, and above all the lawns – she returned to these – were unfenced. James strained his ear for the sounds of a car. How would he know it was the right one? Better wait here until that door behind her opened and the police walked in. He tried to think of the pictures she had come to destroy, but instead of their familiar pallor something neon bright and soda-pop vivid spun into his vision: lime-juice-green lawns and crème-de-menthe foliage, Marga's dream. Nostalgic, lost – canvases by Hopper, Wyeth, Norman Rockwell filled the frame of his mind's eye. American Gothic: an old couple rocking on a gingerbread porch, her parents waiting for her, who would not be back. Was that the car? No . . . Magazine art, *New Yorker* covers, pictures for people who didn't understand art but liked what they liked danced fervently as she talked. Mad Marga, he thought. She did have fervour, only lacked direction, and whose fault was that? Lonely – it had been her loneliness he had loved, he remembered now – why shouldn't she want to go home as Gio had? Fat Gio, proud of his restaurant and calling James *il mio dottore*. James was Marga's *dottore* too, and derelict in his duties.

'Come and visit me there,' she was saying, 'why don't you?' – while the purr of the police car on the drive made James adjust his grip on the gun, which was pointed at her in case there should be a moment's confusion when the cops slipped in the door.

'I will,' he promised before his divided mind could send the signal to the rest of him that the place where he would have a chance to visit her would not be Council Bluffs.

Why Should Not
Old Men Be Mad?

It was a ridiculous occasion. The beginning of the row did nobody credit, and Edward could not for the life of him remember its end. Over the years, his memories of the thing were to curdle, growing spotty and sulphurous, until they put him in mind of the reflections one sees in mirrors which have hung in damp, haughty, old houses and perpetuate their gloom.

The evening got off to a bad start. Jammet's, for decades Dublin's smartest restaurant, had, towards the end, accumulated a stable of rickety old waiters with hamburger faces who that night – here memory sharpened to a knife-edge – snubbed the party's host.

Jim Farrel, a student fresh from the country and unused to restaurants, had chosen to spend half a term's allowance on dinner for four men he didn't know. The guests were Edward, who had just been elected to the Senate, Monsignor Macateer, later to become Bishop of Oglish, a German theologian, and an English Catholic MP who was in Dublin for a conference. The four knew of each other but did not know Farrel, who had led each to suppose that one of the others had asked him to arrange the gathering. His white lies were exposed when he came to pay the bill, and his guests overcome by awkwardness, mirth and doubt as to whether he could possibly have found their conversation worth the expenditure. Had they, they covertly asked each other, sung sufficiently well for their supper? They must, Edward privately supposed, be feeling like an inexperienced young girl who has been treated too sumptuously by a suitor. What, she as they must wonder, would now be expected?

Perhaps it was to bridge this ticklish moment that the German offered a round of brandies and that Edward, feeling light-hearted, resolved to consult Mikey Macateer about his marital problems.

Discreetly, man to man – he had known Mikey since school – he brought up the matter of an annulment. Two annulments. Both Jennifer and he were married. The year was 1958. Was there, he asked Mikey, any chance?

The Monsignor rounded on him like a snake.

Possibly, he had found the evening a strain? The German, an ascetic with advanced ideas, was not the sort of man with whom Mikey felt at ease, and he must have been on pins and needles lest Edward, a Civil-Liberties supporter, let the country down in front of the English M P. Annulments were the last straw.

Mikey's lips had quivered like the cardiogram of a wildly pumping heart. Between them his tongue wavered forth, as he asked in a hiss of enraged and spittly Gaelic whether Edward was deliberately giving scandal to foreigners. Trying for annulments was an erosion of the system, said Mikey. It was a factor for disorder, a time-bomb placed at the heart of Mother Church who, whether Edward knew it or not, was going through risks and trials unknown since the days of Martin Luther.

Tics sucked Mikey's cheeks inwards as though it were being pierced by sewing-pins. Edward, he said, was a fornicator and he a man who called a spade a spade.

'Spayed is what you are,' Edward had answered in English. 'Hiding,' he had shouted, 'behind your dog collar.' The Irish clergy, said Edward, reaching for old invective, were living in the Dark Ages, leaving no choice to the laity but between total abstinence and having six children.

'Sex,' wondered the German doubtfully, 'children?'

'Six,' Edward corrected him.

After that, the level of discourse sank. Appearances ceased to be kept up. Scandal was given, but memory drew a veil. Edward's recollection of the end of the business was a blank. Luckily, he had no further occasion to meet anyone who had been present that evening and his host, Jim Farrel, faded utterly from his ken.

News did, however, continue to reach him of Mikey Macateer's rise. Over the years, the fellow was made a bishop, called to Rome, given a place in the Curia and there alleged to be a man of influence. It stuck particularly in Edward's craw to hear that, after Vatican Two, Macateer became a big progressive, famed for his fight to ditch the cult of abnegation and find the human face of Catholicism. He was hot for reform, it seemed, and instrumental in making annulments easy to get – too late, of course, for Edward and for Jennifer, who was by then so seized up with arthritis that she had had to go and live in Palm Springs.

'Fuck,' mourned Edward when he thought of this.

It was eighteen years after the Jammet's row that someone in Edward's hearing mentioned Macateer as possibly *papabile* – at any rate, a Power in the Vatican, a dexterous string-puller and an *Eminence Verte*. This was at the Irish Embassy in Rome, so Edward allowed for exaggeration. Still, no smoke without fire. There must be some flicker of truth to it. Edward felt green-eyed – well, why wouldn't he? There *he* was, having to turn his mind to retirement and hobbies while that ecclesiastical turncoat slithered upwards in his pride and power. To be sure, churchmen paid a price for their long span of active life: no sex, no kids, loneliness – *what* loneliness? There'd be precious little loneliness for chaps who had made a go of it. Peaking late, they had the best of both worlds in the end. There was Mikey surrounded – Edward supposed he was surrounded – by priestly boot-lickers, pious catamites, a court, and snowed under by invitations.

Edward refused to attend a lunch where the ambassador – a busybody – had hoped to bring the estranged friends together. Having pretended that he had to press on to Venice, he was then obliged to leave the Eternal City earlier than planned. This too stuck in his craw. It wasn't that foolish old business at Jammet's which made him refuse to see Mikey. That was water under the bridge. After eighteen years you buried – or drowned – hatchets. No, no, but, oh, somehow, the invitation had found him in low fettle. He'd been feeling his age. Rome mocked him with memories of old adulteries – it had been a favourite venue for them and, maddeningly, the props were still there: mimosa, *carrozze*, that piss-poor wine that in the old days had not tasted pissy at all. He remembered saying to Jennifer that it was like drinking bottled sunlight.

So, 'No,' he told the embassy chap who rang. 'Sorry.'

It seemed unfair; it seemed *wrong* that Macateer should be reaping what he hadn't sown: esteem, good fellowship and the company of youth, when Edward, who had given so much of himself to so many, was alone.

Two years went by. Then came a letter from Macateer, apparently back in Ireland. It was a summons to visit, and Edward disregarded it. The twit was clearly puffed up with self-esteem. Celibates got that way. Proponents of a married clergy should make use of the point. Hammer it home. Edward thought of saying this in a card to Mikey since *he* was now such a reformer. Instead, he forgot about him.

Weeks later, casting about for gossip with which to enliven a letter to a favourite cousin, he remembered him. Susan was the last attractive female in Edward's entourage and he cherished her with a sad ironic gaiety. Like himself, she suffered from withdrawal symptoms. It wasn't that she or he were withdrawing from anything. No, things were withdrawing from *them* and at such a clip that this time Edward could think of no news to tell her. He fell back on working Mikey's summons into an anecdote and, having done so, began to believe that maybe there *was* more to it than met the eye. Jaundiced spectacles? Perhaps.

'His Grace the Bishop of Oglish,' wrote Edward, 'writes from an ecclesiastical loony-bin somewhere near Athlone, i.e. in the soggy middle of the country, saying he would like a visit. Princely command? Cry for help? What is His Grace doing in a bin in the bog? A Beckettian fix – unless he's running it. But even then what a come-down from the corridors of the Curia where, they say, he was *un très Grand Manitou*. His nicknames tell much: Macchiatelly, because of being smooth on the box, Macateer the Racketeer, inevitably, Mac the Knife. Has someone got their knife into Mikey? I shall go, see and report. Hope I whet your appetite for further bulletins?'

It was all fantasy, including the nicknames – or was it?

Elation at having managed to make something out of nothing led to a doubt that there might be something where he had at first seen nothing. Edward, a virtuoso barrister, had in his prime been able to convince juries of anything he chose. Now, cut off from the medicinal cynicism of day-to-day reality, he found that he could all too easily convince himself.

Satan fodder finds for idle minds – or so Mikey and he had been told in kindergarten.

He wished – God, how he wished – that he was still racked by intimate doubts and choices. For years his letters to Susan had been mined with anguished questions: Should he leave his wife, who would pine incapably if he did, and take off with Mil? Leave Mil for Jennifer? Sell up this house and follow Jennifer to Palm Springs? Return to his pining wife before she died? No alternatives left now. Susan held his hand in a desert awful with the lack of them. Oh shit, oh *shit*! Well, *there* was one function left to him still and quite satisfactory, thanks.

'Life,' he wrote and probed an ear with his pen while wondering what to write next, 'here is as calm as a gold-fish tank with one half-animate inmate: me. A silvered one. My hair pales and drops, as I soon shall myself. Contemporaries drop like flies and my address-book turns into a graveyard guide. I have to keep pencilling out names for fear of gaffes like the one I made with poor Martin Clancy last month at the Yacht Club. "How's Mil?" I asked. He looked at me in shock: "Mil's been dead three years." Had I known? Suppressed and blinked away knowledge? Perhaps. Like black tennis-balls smashed at you across a net, like objects dark against the sun, news like that darkens the mind and sets up a refusal. Silly Milly Clancy – you won't remember, but thirty years ago her beauty was breathtaking – Mil dead? Mil laid down in Glasnevin and rendered to a compost fit to blow half Dublin sky-high. Or just gone? Whoo, like a puff of air. Whee, like the intervocalic Latin *t* that became a *d*, then disappeared: *vita, vida, vie. La vida es un sueño*, so why, as Willy Yeats rightly if rhetorically demanded, should not old men be mad?'

Edward supposed he was being literary, but what the hell? He felt weepy, too, and to yield to *that* would be worse. In one corner of his eye, Milly Clancy lurked in luminous tennis-dress and a rainbow casing of teardrop: like Snow White awaiting a kiss in her glass coffin. Get away, Mil! What else was I – ah, yes, madness and the Case of Mikey Macateer.

Old grudges had dissolved into a ferocious solidarity with Mikey, a possible victim of Vatican foul play. Could he have been nudged from his Curial niche? He could. He could. Priestly machinations were infamous and ditto the ruthlessness of today's youth. Edward was in a position to know, having been edged out of his own firm by his own sons – well, he'd *let* himself be edged out. The three were too dim to make a living on their own, and perhaps he was trying to repay their dead mother by being soft with her sons? Blood was thicker than water, though *they* didn't strike him as having a drop in their veins. Put the three through a mangle and he'd be surprised if anything came out: blood, juice or jism. Plastic men. Their passions were for crosswords, beagling and messing with small intricate boats. Small, mark, nothing on a scale to accommodate the lurch and sway of sea-borne loves. No, tinkering with stalled engines was what they liked. They rarely left the harbour.

To be fair – fairness had been Edward's loadstone – *they* found him trying. His flourish embarrassed them. He knew. He saw. Freesias in his lapel, the length of his cuffs. Even his concern with human rights struck them as spiritual social-climbing. 'Pragmatic' was their favourite word. Economics, they instructed, was what mattered now. No, *not* in the Marxist sense. Forget words like 'left' and 'right'. Ireland had never had it so good. In the convex diminishing-mirrors of their eyes, he saw himself as a sentimental old codger fighting the fights of long ago.

An Americanized generation, they admitted to boredom when not working. Yet all three had married and were, as they were quick to point out, nicer to their wives than Edward had ever been to their mother. So alien were they that if she'd had it in her to take a lover he'd have thought them bastards. She hadn't. Maybe they'd been sired by gamma rays on evenings when she'd been sitting back, legs apart, watching re-runs of *Peyton Place*?

Edward was seized by an urge to see old Mikey Mac who, in another era, used to climb on his shoulders to sneak back in over the seminary wall after the two had stayed out till dawn dancing at a Ceilidh.

Wet furry fields lay like the stomachs of soft animals bared to the sky. The train, with Edward in it, tore masterfully through the flat lands of middle Ireland. He felt zesty and wondered whether Mikey needed help. Edward was still President of Civil Liberties. Had some Lilliputian bureaucrats pinned Mikey down? Ah, look out there for the old war-horse twitch. Edward. Delusions of grandeur! Watch it, do! It was a typical daydream to fancy that you were needed by the powerful. Since Aesop's mouse, God help us, all mice must dream of saving lions. And what worse dreamer than the mouse emeritus?

He took a taxi from the station, arrived unannounced and gave his card to the porter: Senator Edward O'Hourraghan, President of Civil Liberties, hon. sec. of this, that and the other. He was in the honoraries these days, thought of the condition as akin to the DTs: shivery syllables, a ghostly status. He wanted, he told the flunkey, to see the Bishop. The man was a bit ghostly himself: cobweb hair, dandruff powderings, a silhouette from eighteenth-century farce. Which bishop? he asked. How many had they got, then? Edward briskly inquired. 'Oglish,' he bullied, 'Bishop Michael Macateer.' He knew how to inject authority into his voice.

Twenty minutes later he was in an institutional parlour – all angles, vacancy and reflecting surfaces – facing a silver-haired Mikey dressed in velvet pants and the sort of purple poloneck you might expect to find in a Jermyn Street shop. Failing to determine Mikey's status, Edward wondered whether this was trendy wear in the Vatican.

'Are you here for long?' he probed.

Mikey's palms were like powder-puffs and his eyes had the bloom of sloes. How good of Edward to have come, he marvelled, and held Edward's hands between his own as though they were infinitely precious. 'At our age one should hasten to repair bridges, don't you think?' He gazed intently and in a rather Latin way at Edward. 'What'll you have?' he asked. 'Wet your whistle?'

Edward chose whiskey and, when Mikey opted for tea, wondered might the Bishop have come here to dry out discreetly.

A man in a white coat hovered, summoned the porter to bring a trolley with refreshments, then took himself off to a window-seat. Mikey made some inadequate introduction which Edward failed to catch and the man kept looking out of the window in a way which made it unclear whether he was to be included in the conversation. At one point he turned and disconcerted Edward by the energy of his stare. It was targeted on the teacup which Mikey had raised to his lips. Edward, following it, expected to see a palsied quiver, but

Mikey's hand was steady. His complexion did, perhaps, suggest drink? Priests, being denied one outlet, turned traditionally to the other. The surrogate, accepted in Ireland, might shock in Rome. Bloody Eyeties, thought Edward, high on sympathy for Macateer, whose stamina should not – any more than Edward's own – be put in doubt over a matter of tippling. The man in the white coat was about the same age as Edward's sons. What was he? Doctor? Minder? Terrible for old Macateer to be under scrutiny. Edward, on a surge of brotherly feeling, slapped his old sparring partner on the back before the cup was safely returned to its saucer. Drops slopped onto Mikey's trousers and Edward's sleeve. Slow reflexes there, Edward acknowledged. Mikey was getting slow. His own mind was a bit murky suddenly. Was the minder watching *him*? he wondered, but was embarrassed to check.

'Well,' he mustered heartiness. 'It's grand to see you.'

Mikey confessed that he had been hurt that time when Edward had avoided him in Rome. He'd put the ambassador up to issuing the invitation, so the refusal had been something of a slap in the face. 'One needs old friends,' he said sadly. New ones tended not to be disinterested.

Edward couldn't have agreed more. Feeling emotional, he dredged up the old lie about how he couldn't have stayed in Rome that time. Wanted to. Couldn't. Believing himself, he swore that the thing had been out of his hands.

'Oh, I never held it against you,' said Mikey. 'It goes back to that night in Jammet's when I was so bloody-minded. I've often wanted to apologize for that. Times change, eh? New criteria. Besides there were things on my mind. You wouldn't know this, but the lady in question . . .'

'Jennifer.' Edward was annoyed by Mikey's terminology. It came straight from police files. It was a tongs for picking up dirt. 'Jennifer Dooley,' he said firmly.

'Her sons,' said the Bishop, 'were pupils of mine at Gonzaga.'

'I never knew that.'

'They were. Nice boys. Vulnerable. Still, I suppose I was a bit straitlaced. Fighting doubts of my own. The toughest hour comes before the breakthrough, and I took it out on you. I've always regretted that.' Macateer's forthright look seemed a touch too good to be true. 'How is she now?' he asked.

Edward, hardened rather than softened, found himself testing Mikey's apology, mentally fingering it for flaws.

'A nice woman,' said Mikey. Jennifer had never been that. 'How did you say she was?'

Edward hadn't and wasn't going to. There was a sinister symmetry to poor Jennifer's condition. Arthritis sounded like an old penance for making too free with your limbs. She, who frolicked in alien beds and meadows – for a moment he smelled flattened grass – she, whose bum once flashed like milk or mushrooms, shall be confined to a wheelchair in a desert city in the circle of the Californicators. He imagined rows of raddled, leathery, legless old things. Or was Palm Springs in Nevada? Surely not? That name suggested snow. Niveous belly. Snowy thighs. Once smooth as egg-shells – were they scrambled now?

Edward's distress brimmed for Mikey too, who had his own afflictions. Anguished, he found he'd finished the whiskey which he'd been planning to nurse. He hoped drinking in Mikey's presence didn't upset him. Trying to slide the glass out of sight, he found that he'd only succeeded in attracting the attention of the doctor or minder who asked would Edward like a refill.

'No, no.' Edward repudiated excess. 'Thanks, though,' he conciliated and was shocked to receive a wink. The man in the white coat stared with a poker face at Edward then, for a second time, coolly and deliberately winked at him. Edward shifted his gaze hurriedly to Mikey who, sitting with his back to the doctor, was discoursing on how happiness was the goal of marriage, the fleshly bond a holy one and the day fast approaching when the Church would admit a dead marriage to be dead. 'Or so,' he wound up, 'I fervently hope. *I've* been fighting hard for that. Too hard for my own good.'

Edward looked at the whiskey-bottle and saw spots in the amber. Black, like flies congealed, they moved when he shifted his gaze. This new weakness appalled him. Had that man winked or hadn't he? The laity, he heard Macateer state, were far more backward than the clergy. Women, especially, were frightened of divorce.

'Think of farmers' wives in a place like this.' Macateer waved out at lush pasturage beyond the Institution lawn. A cow stared in at Edward, its mouth moving from right to left and back. 'What does divorce mean to *them*? That some young strap could catch their man's fancy and take their place on the farm. Have them put off the land. Evicted. Turned into landless vagrants.' The racial and sexual terrors there, said Macateer, ran deep. The Church had to consider the needs of the bulk of the people, the more traditional as well as those impatient for change.

The maggoty things in the whiskey leaped like letters on a screen. 'Impatient,' Edward heard and decided that Macateer thought that he, Edward, had been impatient because he'd known he'd soon be past it, now *was* past it and could look forward to no new embraces. Macateer mentioned the hare and the tortoise. A judicious clergy would not, said Macateer, and *should* not try to keep up with the wilder elements, the hares . . .

'By the time the tortoise reached the goal,' Edward remarked, 'the hare had probably either left in disgust or gone mad with impatience. You can't please *everyone*.' No sooner was the word 'mad' out of his mouth than he saw his gaffe. You didn't say that word in a madhouse any more than you said 'rope' in the house of a hanged man. Nervously, his eye met the minder's and in confusion he stretched out his glass and accepted the refill he didn't want. Change, said Macateer's imperturbable voice, *would* come. There was no *doctrinal* objection to divorce . . . Edward stopped listening. Could the man really imagine that he wanted to hear all this? That he would find solace in being told *now* that he might as well have left his wife and run off with Jennifer? Could he? In Edward's prime it had been professional suicide in Dublin for a man to defy the Church, and Edward had had no choice but to knuckle under. His needs, it seemed, had been subordinated to those of the wives of randy farmers. To avoid a quarrel he tried to change the subject. 'Tell me about Rome,' he said. 'What's the state of play there? No,' he amended, 'I mean in the Vatican.'

Rome, sweet Rome, was something else; at least for Edward it was. A cruel fleshy town. Mentioning it had brought its crusty flavours to his tongue: meat cooked till it fell off the bone, rosemary twigs tied to the legs of lambs slaughtered when they were no bigger than a cat, spitted skylarks. Jennifer had once confessed to feeling guilt over her greed for these birds so unsportingly netted on their migration southwards. A blithe but not spiritual pleasure, she'd admitted, while wiping flecks of charred songbird from her nose and chin. Shame, she'd reminded shrewdly, gave eating that extra tingle usually peculiar to sex, and she and he, in all that enormous Roman *rosticceria*, would be alone in feeling it: a bond. He had kissed her sucked and greasy fingers.

'Keats isn't our tradition really,' he'd argued.

Open fires, turning spits and flushed faces gave the place a look of old-time visions of hell.

'Eat the carcasses,' a waiter had shouted at them, laughing in sensual empathy. 'They're the tastiest part. Hold them by the beak and chew the heads.'

Edward's mouth was dry with memory and tears pricked at his eyes. In places like that, Jennifer and he found bliss tuned to perfervid pitch by their nervous adulterers' yearnings. It had been on a Roman weekend that they had admitted to each other that they would never make the break.

'So what's the news from the Vatican?' he asked again.

Raising his eyes, he saw that behind Mikey's head the man in the white coat was vigorously shaking his own.

'The news' – Macateer tilted his broad boxer's chin — 'is that I'm giving you a chance to return good for evil.' The chin jutted. It always had. Mikey led with it, but its aggression now was subverted by tremors. 'I take it you're still head of Civil Liberties?'

The man in the white coat could have been directing a tangle of traffic. Stop, menaced his gestures: careful. Or was it deaf-and-dumb language? Maybe *he* was the inmate and Macateer in charge?

'Are you?'

'Yes.'

'In the past, you and I have differed over definitions and indeed over the desirability of freedom, but today,' said the Bishop lucidly, 'I am asking you to help me to regain my own in its basic, physical form.' The word seemed to set off a reflex. 'Fizzz-z-z . . .' he faltered in a spurt of hilarity. 'Physical.' Mirth drained from his face as quickly as it had come. 'I want you,' he ended quietly, 'to get me out of here.'

Edward feared that a laugh would be inappropriate. One had, however, got half-way up his throat.

'You may question my right to ask,' said Macateer. 'It is the right of the helpless.' He jabbed a finger at Edward.

As though reading subtitles, Edward peered to where the man behind seemed now to be exhorting patience. With whom? Was Macateer bonkers, then? And, if he was, then why was he allowed to write *and post* imperious letters? It was an outrage that a man of Edward's age and station should be dragged half-way across the country at a madman's whim. Embarrassing, too.

Yet Macateer was the picture of sanity. He smiled at Edward then, reproaching himself, shook his head. 'I've sprung it on you. Tss.'

The chap in the coat was familiar from somewhere. Where? The puzzle kept popping into the foreground of Edward's mind, distracting him. He wished the chap would leave the room, or else that Mikey would. Then he could ask one about the other.

Mikey, anxious lest Edward be harbouring grudges, was launched on a history of his own doctrinal waverings. Where he had ended up, he told Edward, was in the same boat as himself, with the other side out to get him.

Get whom?

'Me.' Macateer added that, though Edward might think him a Johnny-come-lately to the cause of liberalism, this was far from true. There was a tide in such movements and to anticipate it could only be counter-productive, self-indulgent and, in a sense, yes, mad. Was Edward being called mad now? It seemed he was. Mikey's face had grown supercilious. It reminded Edward of some portrait of a doge. Was it in the Wallace Collection? he wondered, but thought not. His attention kept dodging and scampering. It was the intensity of Mikey's onslaught. Made one back off. 'Voltairian rationalism,' he heard Mikey sneer, was all liberalism could be in the context of the forties and fifties when Edward was a liberal. Later, on the other hand . . . Bullying rhythms drummed. Mikey's fingers formed a knot as taut as a cricket-ball ready to lunge out and bash the bails off all obstacles to Mikey's will. Edward, inevitably reminded of the dogmatic old Mikey, saw that the memory showed, for, perceptibly, the tones softened and gave way to ingratiating ones so wrong for Mikey that Edward, teeth on edge, felt a panicked urge to plead: 'Stop, don't do this to us. Don't humiliate yourself.' Maybe, in fairness, he *should* do this? But wouldn't it be *more* humiliating for Macateer if he did? As a compromise, he tried to catch his eye, but its beam was wavering evasively over Edward's shoulder.

'You don't like me,' said Macateer surprisingly. 'Isn't that a good reason why you *should* help me?' Now his eye did catch Edward's in an iron-blue clench. 'Isn't that the liberal ethic?' he challenged. 'I have served an institution,' said Macateer. 'You fight the tyranny of institutions. What about taking on this one?' He gestured at the walls of the room. He had always admired Edward's gutsiness, he said, which was why he was appealing to him now. In the past Edward had stood up and been counted, defending sacked schoolteachers and other radicals and, at the risk of damaging his practice, held out against a domineering Church.

The bathos made Edward wonder if he was being mocked. 'Are you,' he checked, 'making fun of me?'

'Fun?'

'We achieved so little.'

'You kept the idea of liberty alive.'

The man's face puffed with assurance. What did he believe? Now the man in the white coat was listening with interest. Edward's struggles, said Macateer, reminded him of the dissidents in the Soviet Union.

'You embarrass me,' said Edward. 'We have no Siberia in Ireland.' He laughed at the ridiculousness of this.

'No, but people can,' said Macateer, 'get committed to asylums! Not that the agency which committed *me* was Irish.'

There was a silence. A sweaty gleam, hovering, halo-like, about the Bishop, could come from strain or the stimulus of drugs. The white-coated man guffawed with sudden violence.

'Ah, now, yer Grace, yer not comparing the Vatican to the Kremlin, I hope?' He winked at Edward, who again was shocked.

Macateer ignored him. 'Would Civil Liberties,' he asked Edward, 'take on the Vatican? Just to the extent of opening an inquiry? It would not, you understand, be limited to my case?'

'You've turned against the Church?'

'A certain church.'

'You mean,' Edward pressed incredulously, 'that you would take legal action against . . . some agency . . . in the Vatican?' The man was deranged, he decided with relief and a feeling of let-down. His fighting spirit, roused like an old horse taken too briefly from its paddock, was all a-tremble. He looked at Mikey, an awful old man, the spirit of smug Irish Catholicism personified, and saw no reason why freedom-lovers should fight for him. Mad or sane now, he had in his day been as repressive as he had had the power to be and was unrepentant. Mikey's mind was tidy, his commitment extreme. Once, it had been expedient for the Church to be traditionalist and tough. Now Mikey saw it as wise to move the other way. 'Wise' meant politic.

'I am no defector.' Mikey's eyes were blazing, his cheeks concave. Fragility reached a taut climax in him as in a windblown candle. Edward was responsive to this passion of the flesh as he had not been to Mikey's words. These, however, came grating and panting out in a gravelly torrent. A man loyal to his institution, said Mikey, arguing with the fluency of habit, did not refrain from criticizing it when necessary. Neither did he leave it. He laboured to change it from within. Went *into* labour to produce a new version of it. To leave was easy – and ineffective. Defectors became enemies. 'To stay and struggle,' said Mikey, his eyes bulging painfully, 'is the test of loyalty.' Here Mikey's discourse grew obscure, black, thought Edward, like the tip of a smoking candle-flame. He had been persecuted, it appeared, had roused unworthy passion, courted isolation, trouble, personal animosities which – well, all communities harboured such. Edward must understand. Edward didn't. Conspiracies were hinted at. Mikey smoked and fumed.

Suddenly, the man in the white coat had taken a glass of water from the trolley and, walking over to the quivering Macateer, handed him a coloured pill. 'Mustn't excite yourself,' he admonished. 'He gets worked up,' he told Edward. 'Dangerous at his age, don't you know. Here,' he harried Macateer. 'Remember our agreement?'

Macateer snatched the pill and swallowed it with a gulp of water. 'Sycophant!' he shouted.

The minder went back to his window-seat.

Macateer tilted the back of his head at him. 'Bet you don't know who *he* is? Our genial host: Jim Farrel. Name mean nothing to you?' Macateer's angry eyes stabbed at Edward. 'Had us all to dinner,' he prompted. 'Twenty years ago? Remember? Poured champagne, buttered us up and footed the bill. Throwing a sprat to catch a salmon, mm? He's the original Platonic pragmatist and parasite.' Macateer paused. When he spoke again it was with diminished energy. 'If you help me,' he told Edward, 'Jim'll play ball. He likes to be on a winning team. If you don't . . .' He pointed his thumb downwards.

Farrel winked. 'A joke,' he said. 'His Grace likes to –'

'Toady!' Like a schoolyard insult, the word pebbled over Macateer's shoulder. To Edward he spoke quietly. 'Jim's mum had a hardware shop down the country. A tidy little concern. He has the sensitivity of cast-iron *and* its toughness. *I* found that useful, mind. I took him to Rome with me – aha, you didn't know that? Yes, yes, he was my minion there for years. My catspaw. Forgive the quaint diction. He's a quaint creature. Turned his coat. In the end he helped my enemies certify me. Why not? From his and their point of view, a man who ceases to know his own interest is mad, and I, feeling my time run out, ceased to bide it. Thus they could think that I would be best off in my native island with my old slavery enslaving me. Italian journalists are inquisitive; it was best to get me out of reach. He's tapping his forehead, isn't he?' Macateer, without looking round to where Farrel was indeed making this gesture, mimicked it perfectly. The hand tapping his high papery forehead was covered with raised brown moles. Macateer seemed older and more overgrown by the moment. A loser? 'My crime,' he told Edward, 'was your own failing: intemperateness. Also,' Mikey smiled without gaiety, 'love. Love of my family, which is and was the Church.'

Edward's brain buzzed. His stomach was making itself felt. Drink and excitement were lethal at his age. He should get out of here. But a quick withdrawal could look heartless. Antagonistic forces tugged. Emotionally, he could have been being quartered by wild horses. Sectioned. Minced. Eagerness pulsed in him: that lethal itch to live. Poor bloody Mikey! *Mon semblable, mon frère!* Yes? No? Issues which Edward had long thought settled and jelled beneath the veneer of age's mellowness had begun to toss, jumbled like notions in an adolescent's brain. The sensation was nostalgic and disagreeable.

'Don't excite yerself, now,' said Jim Farrel, perhaps speaking to both old men.

Procrastinating, Edward decided not to catch the train tonight. He'd stay in a local hotel he'd seen touted by the gastronomic guides.

'You're not going?' Mikey was aghast.

'Must.' Edward tapped his watch. 'Only to Ballylea House. I'll come again tomorrow.' This was a false promise. He'd have to see. When he pressed Mikey's hand, it felt like spaghetti: a mess of veins. Mikey's eyes looked at him with equally soft appeal and unearned comradeliness. Not many of us left, Edward. Who's 'us', Mikey?

Farrel took Edward to the front door, then through a portcullis of rain to canvass the car-park for lifts. He dashed back with news that a Dr Ryan would be dining at Ballylea House and could take Edward there.

'Was it you posted his letter to me?' Edward managed to ask as he was being settled into the car.

'It was, yes. He has high hopes of you, Senator.' Farrel's face was a blur magnified by the wet window and his tone a concerned nanny's. Edward wondered would he be mad to involve Civil Liberties in this intricate sub-world. 'Phone if you're coming tomorrow,' Farrel shouted as the car drove off. 'Ask for me, Senator: Jim Farrel.'

Dr Ryan accepted a drink in the hotel bar. He was a fresh-faced gossipy psychiatrist and revealed that Farrel wasn't. Wasn't a psychiatrist? Not even a doctor? Edward, remembering Jammet's, and Farrel's weakness for slipping a rung or so above his station, asked, 'A male nurse, then?'

His guest conciliated. 'You could say that. More of an inmate, actually. *You* wouldn't know, to be sure, but in places like this . . .' The lines, it seemed, were fluid, the outfit run by priests, not doctors. 'Oh, ours is definitely a subsidiary capacity.' He mused. 'Odd customers wash up on Irish shores. Gulf Arab girls come here to study nursing. Our reliable chastity is why. Equally, our pious discretion brings anonymous prelates to the Institution. Enough said,' said Ryan, lowering a lid. Farrel, he admitted, *was* an inmate, though of a special sort. 'Mind, it's not my department. All hearsay.

But it seems they came together from Rome: Master and Man.'

'Surely both can't be mad?' And what, Edward wondered, about the white coat? The pill?

'Farrel's good with patients.' The doctor tee-heed. 'Listen, he was a medical student in his youth. We lay man-traps for men like that. You can't imagine how short-handed we are. So, he's humoured, let have the coat and the parlour. Staff in places like this is impossible to get. I married a local girl myself or I'd never have stayed. Then I like the horses. I'm a country type. But I'm unusual.'

'Is anyone in the Institution clinically mad?'

The doctor made the most of this cue. Was Edward a Laingian? He discoursed on madness, quoted Foucault. On wet nights, it seemed, he read. Sure, wasn't it all relative? A matter of being out of step with your immediate community? And hadn't some societies seen madness as divine? Mind you, Pope's crack about great wits being near to madness had especial relevance in the context of the Church. With abstract men subjected to great pressure – especially now, my God, with all the controversy – you'd *expect* breakdowns, wouldn't you? Moments of uncertainty. The Institution specialized in distinguished key thinkers who came here to recuperate. *Sub rosa.* Much could hinge on their emotional health.

'Not mental?'

'Mental, emotional – some may just need a rest.'

'Or to be kept out of the way?'

The doctor – now on his third whiskey – whispered, 'Ah, now, Senator, mum's the word!'

Could he be a semi-inmate himself? Or was Edward succumbing to an insidious folly: believing himself alone in his sanity in a world of lunatics? Ryan, face fat with alcohol, continued his chat. Important with innuendo, he grew big on it, amplifying gestures, grinning, nudging ribs.

'Ah, but silence is golden, eh, Senator, what?' Edward's title seemed all of a sudden to set off a train of thought, for the face shuttered itself at speed. Ryan's mouth twisted, like a key in a lock, as he revealed that he was anxious about his dinner and had better phone his wife pronto. She was late and the table booked for half an hour since. Sorry, Senator, must be off. Great privilege to meet you. Thanks for the drink.

Later, Edward saw him dodge across the lobby under the wing of a woman. Not acknowledging Edward's wave, he scuttled into the dining-room.

Alone in the bar's dimness, Edward was assailed by memories of the decades – his middle ones – when Dubliners had scuttled from him in droves. The town, when he was not yet a senator but already active in Civil Liberties, had been populated with citizens made in the mould of glove-puppets, each equipped with dissimilar sides to his face. The side for public viewing was pious and non-committal. The private side, a glitter of keyed-up bravery, peered, in the shadow of raised collar and lowered hat, like a rabbit from his hole. 'Keep up the good work, Eddy,' these secret fans hissed furtively. 'We'd back ye all the way if it wasn't for the aul' job, don't ye know, the wife, the kids, the pension. Sure you know what it's like yourself. Cross the priests in this country and you're a goner. But we're with you in spirit. You're doing Trojan work!'

He remembered the public ostracism with a cold shudder which he had never let himself feel at the time. In the heat of the fight, pugnacity kept you going. And his swagger had appealed to women. He had enjoyed, even exploited, being odd man out. Now he would get nothing from it. An old man needed approval, needed the goodwill of acquaintances to tether him to a receding world.

What *right* had Mikey to come whining to him? Let him take his come-uppance. According to his own reckoning, the man who played against the odds was a fool.

And what about Edward's reckoning? Wasn't abandoning a principle a way of letting death steal a pass on you? Was it? It was. You became less yourself. Ah, to hell, Mikey wasn't worth fighting for, and it would be a terrible fight. It could bring Civil Liberties into disrepute and stir up untold scandal. A caper like that could lead to not one but two old men being thought demented.

Edward's bladder was bothering him, and he set off for the gents. Passing the dining-room, he saw Ryan's face duck behind a menu in pretence of non-recognition. The light in the men's room was dusty neon, cold as a twilit sea. In a tidal mirror, the face floating towards Edward was fearful, peppered with the marks of doubt, clenched, shifty, explosive and – it struck him with a slow surge of pleasure – vehemently alive. As he came closer, a pink flush began to give it a healthier glow; the lips parted in amusement and a fist lunged ahead of it, pronging two fingers aloft and erect in a waggling V-sign.

He decided to have a bottle of Château Haut Brion 1970 with dinner. It was good neither for his liver nor for his wallet, but seize the moment, seize the day. He'd drink in it to his own and Mikey's intemperate future.

Next morning he was up early. Nowadays, he scarcely slept anyway, and dreams sparked off by his day's doings were best suppressed. He was aware of them slithering back now beneath a mud of oblivion.

The breakfast-room was a splatter of neon. Tables were ice-floes where guests who last night had stayed too long at the bar flipped open napkins and lowered dispirited walrus faces towards their kippers. Edward, however, was brisk. Purpose enlivened him, and his grapefruit was a zesty pleasure. He chatted with the waiter, deciding to walk to the Institution which, the man assured, was no more than a mile off as the crow flew.

It proved a bracing stroll, and he was breathing pastoral air with relish when, half-way up the Institutional avenue, Jim Farrel emerged from the ambush of a rhododendron.

'I had an idea you mightn't phone,' he reproached. 'Listen, Senator, I need a word with you.'

He needed many, it turned out, for Edward would have to be put in the picture if he was to be of any use to Macateer.

'For his sake,' Farrel appealed, 'you should hear both sides.'

Edward, the old lawyer, had to agree that, if there were indeed sides, he'd better take a look at both. He let himself be led through foliage towards a rustic tea-house. The estate had once belonged to members of the old ruling class and bits of pretty pomp subsisted. A lake, visible from where they sat, was fenced off by wire netting.

What Edward must know, said Farrel, was that the Bishop's folly was not personal. 'Madness' – Farrel's face streamed with excited sweat – 'has the whole bloody Vatican in its grip. It's an infection, Senator: a disease. You'd have to know the place to understand. It's very closed off. Patronage and slavery are rampant. You heard our friend call me a hanger-on and worse. Well, that's what I was, and the place is full of men like me: men who carry other men's briefcases for a decade or so, open car-doors for them, dust down their rosaries, live on hope. Hope is the disease, hope and impatience, and the top men are not immune. *They* hope for something else maybe: the Kingdom of Heaven on earth with freedom to love and live carnally extended to all. A new reformed God comforting His creatures with apples of all knowledge and licence.' Through Farrel's tones came a flicker of quotation marks. Clearly, this was parody of something or anyway an echo.

'Macateer?' wondered Edward.

'Aye. You heard what he said: he used to fight it and then he succumbed to it. That's not uncommon, Senator. Look how the old witch-hunters grew fascinated by the thing they were suppressing. There's scholars will tell you that they invented it, that all we know of witches comes from the witch-hunters' reports and that maybe there were no witches at all.' Farrel grinned shyly. 'You pick up queer lore. Well, to come back to the present, the dream that's haunting the place now is old, too: an old heresy. This time, though, it's biting right into the heart of the Church. Right to the *sanctum sanctorum* – and when that happens who's to condemn it?' Farrel's grin grew wolfish and his eyes glittered with an appetite for scandal. 'They say,' he whispered, 'that in the last couple of years *two* popes had to be knocked off. One for sure was done in. Eliminated for the greater good. Can you credit that, Senator?' Cunning pause. Insinuating smile. How far will you go with me? asked Farrel's long streamer of a face. Flecked with dimples of darkness, it flowed whitely in Edward's troubled vision – the tea-house was dusky, and Farrel's presence had an unsettling effect on him. The chap was actually swaying like a cobra in his excitement, and this impeded Edward's apprehension of what he was saying.

'Men like me,' confided Farrel, 'get to know things that the red hats themselves don't know, let alone the bishops. In a sense, we run the place. Why else would we put up with the sort of shit you saw me take from Macateer? We know our worth and that it depends on not being known. Eh, Senator, can you believe that it was men like myself who arranged for those two popes' disposal – men that I maybe know? Doing someone's bidding, to be sure – but tell me this: what's a head without a hand to do its bidding? It's not much, is it? Listen' – he gripped Edward's arm – 'how do you imagine he was got out? Our friend? Mm? Brought over here? By whom? Why? I'll tell you: it was I did it and for his own good. For his safety. Better a spell in the bin than what *can* happen, mm? To be sure, he's in no state to appreciate this.' Farrel paused, waited, but Edward had nothing to say to him. 'You'll have guessed,' the fellow went on, 'that there are factions. What you mightn't guess is how ruthless the fight has to be. No holds barred. The dreamers *have* to be stopped. He – our friend – is the one who taught me that. He was an institution man himself. Trained me up to think like him. Well, it's common sense: when you're afloat in a boat you don't drive a hole in its bottom and you don't let anyone else do it, either. Right? But then he joined the dreamers: started wanting the fruits of eternity in the here and now. Like those popes I mentioned. No need to name names. Impatience, Senator, is a hazard of the profession. Listen, sit down, it's only fair to hear me out. I want to make sure you have things clear. Then you can judge. Sit down, sit down. Have you understood, Senator, that the man in there,' Farrel gestured in the direction of the Institution, hidden behind trees, 'that the Macateer in there is a changeling?'

'I've got to go.'

'I'm speaking metaphorically.'

'Let me pass.'

'In a moment, a wee moment, there's plenty of time.'

'I have a tight schedule.' Edward waved his wrist and watch.

'What's madness, you may ask?' Farrel thrust his face into Edward's, barring his exit from the tea-house. 'Maybe its worst strain is altruism?'

'Let's discuss this later. I want to see Macateer now.'

'You're suspicious of me?' An urchin's humour twiddled at the corners of Farrel's mouth. 'These things are hard to take in.' The cobra sway of Farrel's head made Edward's spin. Right, left, right swayed Farrel, like a goalie guarding his goal. He was in fact guarding the door. 'What have I to gain by hurting you?'

'Is that a threat?'

'Senator!' Farrel was every inch the reproachful nurse – nanny or nursery-school teacher. 'It is because of my deep respect for you,' he spoke with formality, 'that I'm appealing to you on his behalf.

He had to be made to see sense first, *then* restored to his former position.'

'So that he'll restore you to yours?' But Edward was not interested in this dialogue. Its premises were absurd. On the other hand, he hesitated to push past the man, fearing to let things get physical. He wondered would anyone hear him if he were to shout. No, probably not. 'I need,' he improvised, 'to go to the bathroom.'

'Take a leak in the bushes.'

'That's not what I need.'

'O K then, O K.' Farrel, a policeman's grip on Edward's elbow, walked him in custody back towards the avenue. 'First we must talk sense to him,' he explained, while pushing foliage out of Edward's path, 'then help him legally. He has a strong case, but must be persuaded to behave with prudence. Otherwise, things will just start up again the same way. We'll be back to square one. The Progressives are just not going to be let wreck the Church. I wish I had more time to make this clear to you, Senator. I know you find it hard to believe. The new is strange and the strange seems mad – but ours is a time of polarities. You, an old liberal and a man of the middle, owe it to us to hold the ring.' In his excitement, Farrel was backing Edward into brambles and had made him lose his balance. 'Oh, Jesus, I'm sorry,' he shouted and caught the lurching Edward in his arms. 'Steady now, Senator. You don't think *I'd* hurt you, now do you, surely? Me?'

'Why not you? Who are you anyway?'

'I'm your spiritual son. I picked you out twenty years ago.'

'What rubbish.'

'Not rubbish. You remember the dinner at Jammet's? You must. You do. The Bishop mentioned it yesterday. Well, why do you think I gave it? I'd picked you out: you and him. You represented the two sides of my tradition: the Irish heritage. I wanted to apprentice myself. I was looking for a mentor. My father died early, you know. Anyway, he was a limited man. I had ambitions. I wanted short cuts: an adoptive father. One adopted by me who could instruct me, give me a leg up. I planned to get to know you and the Monsignor, as he then was, both. That's why I gave the dinner. The two foreigners were bait. I knew you'd want to meet them – well, I hardly hoped you'd want to meet *me*. But, normally, you should have extended some hospitality after accepting mine. I counted on that. If it hadn't been for the fight you had with Macateer – you'll remember that? – it would have worked. As it was, I had to choose between the two of you right off. I could have brought you home in a taxi – drunk as you were. But your wife would have been there. She wouldn't have let me stay. So I plumped for him, stayed on, flattered him, became his factotum. Secretary. Well, you know all that. But I've often wondered what it would have been like if you'd been my patron. Here we are. You said you needed a bathroom.'

They had reached the door of the Institution.

'I want a taxi,' said Edward. 'I'm leaving.' He couldn't bear to see Macateer now, or indeed anyone else. The fumes of Farrel's unbalanced eagerness made him feel unbalanced himself. It was like getting drunk off another man's breath. He had to be alone for a while.

'He's expecting you. He'll be disappointed. At least say "hello".'

'I'm too old for all this.'

'Too old to turn away from it. The young don't need you. Do your sons need you?'

Edward was astounded at the chap's knowing insolence. Had he been ferreting out information? Gossip? Into that madhouse he was resolved not to put foot.

'I'm going.' He turned, stepped down some steps, hastened, as he heard Farrel come after him and, losing his footing, fell and rolled down the rest of the flight. Feeling the fellow try to pick him up – his leg ached where he had perhaps pulled a muscle – he was impelled by pain and fury to lunge for the bloody ass's face. His knuckles hit something hard – teeth perhaps? – and he felt blood on his fist. Was it his own? He could have wept with exasperation. Feeling himself being further manhandled, he lunged again and realized that he had managed to break his own glasses. Splinters ran into his palm and he could see nothing but blur. Voices reached him confusingly.

'What's up? What's it now? What's the matter?'

'. . . gone berserk. Here, give me a hand.'

'Who is it?'

'A visitor. I know him. Gently now.'

'Who did you say?'

'Drunk?'

'. . . do himself an injury – or us. A friend of Farrel's, is he?'

'What set him off? Here, Pat, Joe, we need help. Those buggers are never there when you need them.'

'Quiet now, Senator . . . need to give him a shot of something. Tough old bastard, isn't he? Music in the old bones yet, what?'

'A damn sight too much. What was it you said . . .?'

'Off his head – doting.' That was Farrel's voice.

'A shot of something. Someone call Dr Ryan.'

Struggling and captive like a newborn infant, Edward felt himself carried in the door.

Will You Please Go Now

Lost among the demonstrators was a rain-sodden dog. Up and down it ran, rubbing against anonymous trousers and collecting the odd kick. It was a well-fed animal with a leather collar but was quickly taking on the characteristics of the stray: that festive cringe and the way such dogs hoop their spines in panic while they wag their shabby tails.

'Here boy! Come – ugh, he's all muddy. Down, sir, get away! Scram! Tss!'

People threw chocolate wrappers and potato-crisp packets which the dog acknowledged from an old habit of optimism while knowing the things were no good. It was tired and its teeth showed in a dampish pant as though it were laughing at its own dilemma.

Jenny Middleton, a mother of two, recognized the crowd's mood from children's parties.

'Don't tease him,' she said sharply to a dark-skinned young man who had taken the animal's forepaws in his hands and was forcing it to dance. The dog's dazed gash of teeth was like a reflection of the man's laugh. 'Here,' she said, more gently, 'let me see his tag. There's a loudspeaker system. It shouldn't be hard to find his owner.'

'I'll take him,' said the man at once, as though, like the dog, he had been obedience-trained and only awaited direction. 'I will ask them to announce that he has been found.' Off he hared on his errand, like a boy-scout eager for merit. One hand on the dog's collar, he sliced through the crowd behind a nimbly raised shoulder. 'I'll be back,' he called to Jenny, turning to impress this on her with a sharp glance from yellowish, slightly bloodshot eyes.

He was the sort of man whom she would have avoided in an

empty street – and, to be sure, she might have been wrong. He was friendly. Everyone at the rally was. Strangers cracked jokes and a group carrying an embroidered trade-union banner kept up a confident, comic patter. The one thing she wasn't sure she liked were the radical tunes which a bald old man was playing on his accordion. They seemed to her divisive, having nothing to do with the rally's purpose. When the musician's mate brought round the hat, she refused to contribute. 'Sorry,' she told him when he shook it in front of her. 'I've no change.' Turning, she was caught by the ambush of the dusky young man's grin. He was back, breathing hard and shaking rain from his hair.

'The dog will be OK,' he assured her. 'The authorities are in control.'

This confidence in hierarchy amused her. The next thing he said showed that it was selective.

'They,' he nodded furtively at the musicians, 'come to all rallies. I am thinking maybe they are the police? Musicians, buskers: a good disguise?' He had a shrill, excited giggle.

'There are plenty of ordinary police here,' she remarked, wondering whether he was making fun of her. She felt shy at having come here alone in her Burberry hat and mac. The hat was to protect her hair from torch drippings and was sensible gear for a torch-light procession. But then, might not sense be a middle-class trait and mark her out?

'Bobbies,' he said, 'are not the danger. I am speaking of the undercover police. The Special Branch. They have hidden cameras.'

'Oh.'

She eased her attention off him and began to read the graffiti on the struts of the bridge beneath which their section of the procession was sheltering. It was raining and there was a delay up front. Rumours or joke-rumours had provided explanations for this. The levity was so sustained as to suggest that many marchers were embarrassed at having taken to the streets. Old jokes scratched in concrete went back to her schooldays: *My mother made me a homosexual*, she read. *Did she?* goes the answer, conventionally written in a different hand. *If I get her some wool will she make me one too?* There was the usual Persian – or was it Arabic – slogan which she had been told meant *Stop killings in Iraq!* The man beside her could be an Arab. No. More likely an Indian.

'I know them,' he was saying of the secret police. 'We know each other. You see I myself come to all rallies. Every one in London.'

'Are you a journalist?'

'No. I come because I am lonely. Only at rallies are people speaking to me.'

Snap! She saw the trap-click of his strategy close in on her: his victim for the occasion. It was her hat, she thought and watched his eyes coax and flinch. It had singled her out. Damn! A soft-hearted woman, she had learned, reluctantly, that you disappointed people less if you could avoid raising their hopes. Something about him suggested that a rejection would fill him with triumph. He did not want handouts, conversational or otherwise, but must solicit them if he was to savour a refusal.

A graffito on the wall behind him said: *I thought Wanking was a town in China until I discovered Smirnov.* Don't *laugh*, she warned herself – yet, if she *could* think of a joke to tell him, mightn't it get her off his hook? Would Chinese laugh at the Smirnov joke, she wondered. Probably they wouldn't, nor Indians either. Wankers might. They were solitary and the solitary use jokes to keep people at bay.

'You see,' he was saying, 'I am a factory worker but also an intellectual. In my own country I was working for a newspaper but here in the factory I meet nobody to whom I can talk. Intellectuals in London are not inviting working men to their homes. I am starved for exchange of stimulating ideas.' His eye nailed a magazine she was carrying. 'You, I see, are an intellectual?'

'Goodness, no.' But the denial was a matter of style, almost a game which it was cruel to play with someone like him. She had never known an English person who would admit to being an intellectual. In India – Pakistan? – wherever he came from it would be a category which deserved honour and imposed duties. Denying membership must strike him as an effort to shirk such duties towards a fellow member in distress.

Her attempts to keep seeing things his way were making her nervous and she had twisted her sheaf of fliers and pamphlets into a wad. Am I worrying about *him*, she wondered, or myself? Perhaps even asking herself such a question was narcissistic? Objectivity too might be a middle-class luxury. How could a man like this afford it? He was a refugee, he was telling her now, a Marxist whose comrades back home were in prison, tortured or dead. Perhaps his party would take power again soon. Then he would go home and have a position in the new government. *Then* English intellectuals could meet him as an equal. He said this with what must have been intended as a teasing grin. She hadn't caught the name of his country and was embarrassed to ask lest it turn out to be unfamiliar. It would have to be a quite small nation, she reasoned, if he was hoping to be in its government. Or had *that* been a joke?

'We're moving.' She was relieved at the diversion.

The trade-union group started roaring the Red Flag with comic gusto and the procession ambled off. He was holding her elbow. Well, that, she supposed, must be solidarity. The rally was connected with an issue she cared about. She did not normally take to the streets and the etiquette of the occasion was foreign to her.

'*Let cowards mock*', came the jovial Greater London bellow from up front, '*And traitors sneer . . .*'

'I'm as foreign here as he is,' she decided and bore with the downward tug at her elbow. He was small: a shrivelled man with a face like a tan shoe which hasn't seen polish in years. Dusky, dusty, a bit scuffed, he could be any age between thirty and forty-five. His fingers, clutching at her elbow bone, made the torch she had bought tilt and shed hot grease on their shoulders. She put up her left hand to steady it.

'You're married.' He nodded at her ring. 'Children?'

'Yes: two. Melanie and Robin. Melanie's twelve.'

The embankment was glazed and oozy. Outlines were smudged by a cheesy bloom of mist, and reflections from street-lights smeary in the mud for it was December and grew dark about four. Across the river, the South Bank complex was visible still. He remarked that you could sit all day in its cafeteria if you wanted and not be expected to buy anything. His room, out in the suburbs, depressed him so much that on Sundays he journeyed in just to be among the gallery- and theatre-goers, although he never visited such places himself.

'But galleries are cheap on Sundays,' she remonstrated. 'Maybe even free?'

He shrugged. Art – bourgeois art – didn't interest him. It was – he smiled in shame at the confession – the opulence of the cafeteria which he craved. 'Op*u*lence,' he said, stressing the wrong syllable so that she guessed that he had never heard the word pronounced. 'It is warm there,' he explained. 'Soft seats. Nice view of the river. Some of the women are wearing scent.'

On impulse and because it was two weeks to Christmas, she invited him to join her family for lunch on the 25th.

When the day came, she almost forgot him and had to tell Melanie to lay an extra place just before he was due to arrive. His name – he had phoned to test the firmness of her invitation – was Mr Rao. He called her Mrs Middleton and she found the formality odd after the mateyness of the rally when he had surely called her Jenny? Their procession, headed for Downing Steet, had been turned back to circle through darkening streets. Mounted police, came the word, had charged people in front. Several had been trampled. Maimed perhaps? No, that was rumour: a load of old rubbish. Just some Trots trying to provoke an incident. Keep calm. Then someone heard an ambulance. An old working man gibbered with four-letter fury but the banner-bearers were unfazed.

'Can't believe all you hear, Dad,' they told him.

Mr Rao tugged at Jenny's arm as though he had taken her into custody: the custody of the Revolution. 'You see,' he hissed, 'it is the system you must attack, root and branch, not just one anomaly. There are no anomalies. All are symptoms.' He was galvanized. Coils of rusty hair reared like antennae off his forehead. 'Social Democrats,' he shouted, 'sell the pass. They are running dogs of Capitalism. I could tell you things I have seen . . .' Fury restored him and she guessed that he came to rallies to revive a flame in himself which risked being doused by the grind of his working existence. He laughed and his eyes flicked whitely in the glow from the torches as he twitted the young men with the trade-union banner in their split allegiance. A Labour Government was loosing its police on the workers. 'Aha!' he hooted at their discomfiture. 'Do you see? Do you?' His laughter flew high and quavered like an exotic birdcall through the moist London night.

*

'You remember that demo I went to?' she reminded Melanie. 'Well, I met him there. He's a refugee and lonely at Christmas. A political refugee.'

'Sinister?' inquired her husband who'd come into the kitchen to get ice cubes, 'with a guerrillero grin and a bandit's moustache? Did he flirt with you?'

This sort of banter was irritating when one was trying to degrease a hot roasting pan to make sauce. She'd just remembered too that her mother-in-law, who was staying with them, was on a salt-free diet. Special vegetables should have been prepared. 'Did you lay the place for him?' she asked Melanie.

The girl nodded and rolled back her sleeve to admire the bracelet she'd got for Christmas. Posing, she considered her parents with amusement.

Jenny's husband was looking for something in the deep freeze. 'He did, didn't he?' he crowed. 'He flirted with you?'

She should have primed him, she realized. James was sensitive enough when things were pointed out to him but slow to imagine that other people might feel differently to the way he did. Mr Rao would be hoping for a serious exchange of ideas between men. Stress serious. He had been impressed when she told him that James, a senior civil servant, was chairman of a national committee on education. But now here was James wearing his sky-blue jogging suit with the greyhound on its chest – a Christmas present – all set to be festive and familial. He was a nimble, boyish man who prided himself on his youthfulness.

'Will Mr Rao disapprove of us?' he asked puckishly and tossed his lock of grey-blond hair off his forehead.

'Listen, he's a poor thing.' Jenny was peeved at being made to say this. 'Be careful with him, James. Can anyone see the soy sauce? I've burnt my hand. Thanks.' She spread it on the burn then went back to her roasting pan. Melanie, darling, could you do some quick, unsalted carrots for your grandmother? Please.'

'Better do plenty,' James warned. '*He* may be a vegetarian. Lots of Indians are.'

'God, do you think so? At Christmas.'

'Why not at Christmas? You'd think we celebrated it by drinking the blood of the Lamb.'

'People do,' said Melanie. 'Communion. There's the doorbell.'

'I'll go. Keep an eye on my pan.'

In the hall Jenny just missed putting her foot on a model engine which James had bought for five-year-old Robin and himself. An entire Southern Region of bright rails, switches, turntables and sidings was laid out and there was no sign of Robin. Did James dream of being an engine-driver, an aerial bomber or God? Or was it some sexual thing like everything else? Through the Art Nouveau glass of the door, she deduced that the blob in Mr Rao's purple hand must be daffodils, and wished that there was time to hide her own floral display which must minimize his gift.

'You were mean, horrible, appalling.'

'*He* is appalling.'

'Shsh! Listen, please, James, be nice. Try. Look, go back now, will you? They'll know we're whispering.'

'*I*'m not whispering.'

'Well you should be. He'll hear.'

'Jenny, you invited him. Try and control him. He has a chip a mile high on his . . .'

'Well, allow for it.'

'Why should I?'

'You're his host.'

'He's my guest.'

'God! Look, get the plum pud alight and take it in. I'll get the brandy butter.'

'If he suggests Robin eat this with his fingers, I'll . . .'

'Shush, will you? He doesn't understand children.'

'What does he understand? How to cadge money?'

'He didn't mean it that way.'

'He bloody did. Thinks the world owes him a living.'

'Well, doesn't it? Owe everyone I mean.'

'My dear Jenny . . .'

'Oh, all *right*. Here.'

She put a match to the brandy-soaked pudding so that blue flames sprang over its globe making it look like a scorched, transfigured human head. 'Go *on*. Take it while it's alight.' She pushed her husband in the direction of the dining-room and stood for a moment pulling faces at the impassive blankness of the kitchen fridge. Then she followed with the brandy butter.

Later, she came back to the kitchen to clean up. Vengefully, she let the men and her mother-in-law cope with each other over the coffee which their guest had at least not refused. He *had* refused sherry, also wine, also the pudding because it had brandy on it and had seemed to feel that it was his duty to explain why he did so and to point out the relativity of cultural values at the very moment when Robin's grandmother was telling the child how to pick fowl high.

'Only *two* fingers, Robin,' she'd been demonstrating daintily, 'never your whole hand and only pick up a *neat* bone.'

'We,' Mr Rao scooped up mashed chestnuts with a piece of bread, 'eat everything with our hands.' He laughed. 'There are millions of us.'

The anarchy of this so undermined Robin's sense of what might and might not be done on such an extraordinary day as Christmas that he threw mashed chestnuts at his grandmother and had to be exiled from the table. The older Mrs Middleton was unamused. Mr Rao bared his humourless, raking teeth.

'You are strict with your children,' he said, 'in imparting your class rituals. This is because as a people you still have confidence and prize cohesion. Maybe now you must relax?'

Nobody chose to discuss this. Doggedly, the family helped each other to sauce and stuffing and Mr Rao began to use his knife and fork like everyone else. A diffidence in him plucked at Jenny who saw that the incident with Robin had been meant as a joke: a humorous overture to the member of the family whom he had judged least likely to reject him. But now Robin himself was rejected, exiled to his room, and disapproval of Mr Rao hung unvoiced and irrefutable in the air. Seen by daylight, he was younger than she had supposed at the rally. His was a hurt, young face, puffy and unformed with bloodshot eyes and a soft, bluish, twitching mouth. He wanted to plead for Robin but could only talk in his magazine jargon. Perhaps he never spoke to people and knew no ordinary English at all? She imagined him sitting endlessly in the South Bank cafeteria reading political magazines and staring at the river.

'Pedagogical theory, you see . . .' he started and James, to deviate him – Robin's exile had to last at least ten minutes to placate his grandmother, interrupted with some remark about a scheme for facilitating adult education with which he was concerned.

'It's designed for people who didn't get a chance to go to university in the first instance,' said James. 'We give scholarships to deserving . . .'

'Could you give me one?' Mr Rao leaned across the table. 'Please. Could you? I am needing time to think and that factory work is destroying my brain. Have you worked ever on an assembly line?'

'You may certainly apply,' James told him. 'It's open to all applicants.'

'No.' Mr Rao spoke excitedly and a small particle of mashed chestnut flew from his mouth and landed on James's jogging suit. His words, spattering after it, seemed almost as tangible. 'No, no,' he denied, nervous with hope. 'You see I apply before for such things and never get them. Inferior candidates pass me by. Here in England, there is a mode, a ritual, you see. It is like the way you educate your son.' Mr Rao's mouth twisted like a spider on a pin. 'You teach him to give signals,' he accused. 'To eat the chicken *so* – and then his own kind will recognize and reward him. I give the wrong signals so I am always rejected.' He laughed sadly. 'Merit is not noted. In intellectual matters this is even more true. Examiners will take a working-class man only if they think he can be absorbed into their class. I cannot.'

'Then perhaps,' said James, 'you are an unsuitable applicant?'

'But the university,' pleaded Mr Rao, 'is not a caste system? Not tribal surely? You cannot afford to exclude people with other ways of being than your own. Even capitalism must innoculate itself with a little of the virus it fears. Intellectual life' – Mr Rao swung his fork like a pendulum – 'is a dialectical process. You must violate your rules,' he begged. 'Isn't that how change comes? Even in English law? First someone breaks a bad old law; then a judge condones the breaking and creates a precedent. I have read this. Now *you*,' Mr Rao pointed his fork at James, 'must break your bureaucratic rule. Give me a scholarship. Be brave,' he pleaded. The fork fell with a clatter but Mr Rao was too absorbed to care. 'Give,' he repeated, fixing James with feverish eyes as if he hoped to mesmerize him. The eyes, thought Jenny, looked molten and scorched like lumps of caramel when you burned a pudding. The fork was again swinging to and fro and it struck her that Mr Rao might not be above using hypnotism to try and make James acquiesce to his will.

She leaned over and took the fork from his fingers. He let it go. His energies were focused on James. The eyes were leeches now: animate, obscene. Melanie and her grandmother were collecting plates. They were outside the electric connection between the two men. Murmuring together, they seemed unaware of it. James's mouth tightened. Mr Rao, Jenny saw, was in for a rocket. But the man was conscious only of his own need. It was naked now. He was frightened, visibly sweating, his nails scratched at the table cloth. He wiped his face with a napkin.

'Men in lower positions must obey rules,' he told James. '*They* will not let me through. Only you can make an exception. Is not the spirit of your scheme to let the alienated back into society? I am such a man,' he said with dramatic intonation. 'I,' he said proudly, 'am needy, alienated, hard working and well read. Do you not believe I am intelligent? I could get references, but my referees,' he laughed his unhappy laugh, 'are tending to be in gaol: a minister of my country, the rector of my university. Oh, we had an establishment once.'

'Then perhaps,' said James, 'you understand about the need to eliminate personal appeals? Nepotism: the approach which corrupts a system. Did you,' asked James with contempt, 'pick my wife up at that rally because you knew who she was? Wait!' He held Jenny's hand to stop her talking. 'I'm quite well known. A number of people there could have recognized and pointed her out to you. A man like you is ruthless, isn't he? For a higher aim, to be sure.' James spoke with derision. 'No doubt you feel you matter more than other people?'

The stuffing had gone out of Mr Rao. His head sank. His mouth, a puffy wound mobile in his face, never settled on an emotion with confidence. Even now there was a twitch of humour in its gloom. 'Oh,' he said listlessly, 'many, many personal appeals are granted in this country. But it's like I said: I don't know the signals. I am an outsider here.' He stood up.

'Please!' Jenny wrenched her wrist from her husband's grip. 'Mr Rao! You're not going? There's pudding. The meal isn't over at all.'

133

But he had only stood up to welcome Robin who, released from his room by his grandmother, was returning in a haze of smiles and sulks. For the rest of the meal, attention was gratefully divided between the child and the food. It was Christmas, after all.

The dishwasher was on. Its noise drowned his approach and added urgency to the hand she felt landing on her arm.

'Jenny!' Mr Rao's shrewd, nervous face peered into hers. 'I go now. I am thanking you and . . .' Words, having betrayed him all day, seemed to be abandoning him utterly. 'Sorry,' he said as perfunctorily as Robin might have done. 'It is not true what your husband said.'

'Of course not. I'm sorry too – but I'm glad you came.' She smiled with a guilty mixture of sorrow and relief. After all, what more could she do? She gave him her hand.

He didn't take it. 'I appreciated this,' he said too eagerly. 'Being in a family. You know? Mine is a people who care a lot about family life. I miss it. That was why meeting little Robin, I . . .'

She thought he was apologizing. 'It's not important.'

'No, no. I know that with children things are always going wrong and being mended quickly. That is the joy of dealing with them. I miss children so much. Children and women – will you invite me again?'

She was astonished. Unaccountably, she felt a stab of longing to help him, to visit the unmapped regions where he lived: eager, vulnerable and alone, with no sense of what was possible any more than Robin had, or maybe great, mad saints. But how could she? The dishwasher had finished a cycle and begun another. It was so loud now that she could hardly hear what he was saying. He seemed to be repeating his question.

'We're going away for a while in January,' she began evasively. 'Skiing . . .' But evasion wouldn't do for this man. She looked him in the eye. 'I can't invite you,' she said. 'James and you didn't hit it off. You must realize that.'

'Will you meet me in town? I'll give you my number.'

'No.'

'Please.'

'Mr Rao . . .'

The wound of his mouth was going through a silent-movie routine: pleading, deriding, angry, all at once. 'The poor have no dignity,' he said, shocking her by this abrupt irruption of sound. 'They must beg for what others take.'

Suddenly, he had his arms around her and was slobbering, beseeching and hurting her in the hard grip of his hands. The sounds coming from him were animal: but like those of an animal which could both laugh and weep. One hand had got inside her blouse. 'A woman,' he seemed to be repeating, 'a family ... woman ...' Then a different cry got through to her: 'Mummy!'

Melanie, looking horrified, stood next to them. The dishwasher, now emptying itself with a loud gurgle, made it impossible to hear whether she had said anything else. Behind her stunned face bobbed her grandmother's which was merely puzzled. The older Mrs Middleton was a timorous lady, slow to grasp situations but constantly fearful of their not being as she would like.

'Mother!' yelled Melanie a second time.

Mr Rao, deafened by lust, loneliness or the noise of the dishwasher, was still clinging to Jenny and muttering incomprehensible, maybe foreign, sounds. She heaved him off and spoke with harsh clarity to his blind, intoxicated face.

'I'm sorry,' she said. 'I'm sorry. But will you please go now. Just leave.'

Bought

In the square rose a concrete island embellished by three trees which in winter were as bare as masts. This was the habitat of a group of winos who rarely left it. When one did it was doubtfully and at an uneven gait: first foot probing, body plunging after at a sailor's lurch. The winos wore layers of cast-off suits rounded by wear but solid enough to have had their earliest airings on bankers' backs. There was parody in the way they waved their bottles and demanded alms.

'*Merci, petite dame, merci. Monsieur*, can you spare a few *centimes* for a poor drunk who needs to get drunker? Well go shit on yourself then, dumb American!'

Americans were drawn to this square by a plaque stating that Henry Miller had lived here before them. They sat beneath his patronage in a glassed-in café. Outside, on their island, the winos made broad, drowning gestures, waved their arms and sometimes gargled methylated spirits to which they set a match, throwing back their heads so that their open mouths were parallel to the sky and great sheets of flame sprang from them. This was a performance and, if watchers did not pay, the abuse could turn violent. Quickly learning how little to give, the Americans forked out with disgust and shame.

'It's horrible. Don't they ever injure themselves?'

'Sure they do. The *patron* here was telling me that they had to rush one off to hospital the other night. There have been several casualties.'

'You could say that their whole life is a kind of destruction.'

'Like a lot of people's. Listen, I've known casualties . . .'

The Americans always got back to talking about themselves. They were riddled with self-doubt. But doubt is a condition for love and they had hopes as wild as the gestures of the flame-eating winos.

Finically, they assessed their past.

'I was someone's concubine for five years,' a young woman stated. 'I let him define me. It was my own fault.'

'Are you a psychic casualty?'

'I think I'm finding myself,' the young woman stated. 'My name is Jane.'

'Looking for a Tarzan?' a man asked.

'Maybe I am Tarzan?' she smiled. She was wearing a jungle suit from the Galeries Lafayette, price four hundred francs. It had been advertised in *Elle*. But on other days she had come to the café wearing tailormade suits cut with the elegance of some years before and there was an air about her as though she might have money. Not much, perhaps, but some.

'I like your cartridge belt,' said a girl. 'Did it come from the Bagagerie?'

Jane took it off. 'Take it.'

'I didn't mean that.'

'I mean it.' Jane buckled it on the girl. 'I'm tied down by things. Too many. Someone's even lent me an apartment. Here, near the square. People always lend me things. If you look rich they'll lend and the more they lend the richer you look. The trick is getting started. In my case it was chance. I'm turning into an adventuress. I should hook a rich man.'

'Do you want to?' someone asked and Jane said she didn't know. She adored self-analysis but the self, like the borrowed possessions, changed.

A cleaning woman came with the apartment.

'You're the only French person I know here,' Jane had said to her just now before coming out. 'Imagine. The only Parisienne.'

The woman said she was French all right. One hundred per cent, Madame, but not Parisienne. No. Her mother came from Lille and she herself lived in the outer suburbs and spent hours every day commuting.

'*Métro, boulot, dodo,*' she said. 'Work, sleep, commute. It's no life.' She had four children and a mouth full of gold stumps. She had been trying for months to get proper teeth from the Sécurité Sociale. 'They say cleaning women don't need them,' she told Jane. 'Smiling has to be part of your job for you to get priority.'

'Have a drink,' Jane offered.

The cleaning woman didn't drink. She started to tell Jane about her life but Jane couldn't bear to listen. What could you *do* for such people? Nothing, she told herself and rushed out to sit in the café. Nothing at all. She began a letter describing the cleaning woman and their upsetting conversation.

Jane wrote enormous numbers of letters. She wrote to people with whom she might stay that summer. She also wrote to the man whose concubine she had been. 'I'm slumming,' she wrote, 'living in squalor. I go to funny little restaurants and I'm writing this in a café full of Americans with hair like poodles who say they were draft-dodgers and an African who's lecturing another African on religion and a raggletaggle of French. The French,' she wrote, 'seem grim, probably because they'll never be able to get away as the rest of us do. It'll be *métro, boulot, dodo* for them for the rest of their lives. They know it and it gives their mouths that mean French look.'

She licked the envelope then wiped her tongue in a handkerchief. There was no FDA here to check on the glue they put on envelopes.

'The bit in the horse's mouth controls the animal,' the African at the next table told his companion, 'as the word of God controls the believer. Ships though they are great are controlled by a small rudder. So too the tongue though small.'

Fritz came in and leaned on the café counter. Jane smiled and he came over to her table.

'OK if I join you?'

'Sure.'

Fritz was a painter with some claim to be Viennese and some to be American. Jane thought he might be falling in love with her.

'I'm not interested in love,' she told him. 'Nature meant it to be a phase, a functional moment. But people let it unbalance their lives. Like youth. I want to know who I am and settle down. I want to *do* something.'

'*I'*m not a youth-worshipper,' said Fritz. 'They'd better not get in my way.'

He talked about his painting and about an exhibition someone was letting him have. The arrangements were unsatisfactory. Everything seemed wrong. His lower lip quivered. He kept wiping it with his handkerchief and she saw how he would arouse distrust in any businessman. How had he ever persuaded anyone to lend him a gallery?

'I'm not expecting to be reviewed,' he told her. 'You have to pay bribes if you want that.' There was to be no *vernissage* and the gallery was supplying no staff. 'I've got to find people to take turns sitting there,' he said. 'Just to hand out catalogues and see that nobody throws up on the carpet or rips off the paintings.' He had an explosive, humourless laugh.

'I'll give you a few afternoons,' Jane offered.

'Bring something to read,' he warned, 'there won't be many visitors.'

But she could tell he had secret hopes. Someone might just drift in. A buyer. A critic. Fritz was throwing his bread upon the waters. To do more, he told her, would be going along with a rotten, corrupt system.

'Even if I had the money,' he told her, 'I wouldn't bribe. I wouldn't advertise. I don't want success at any price. I don't want it at a price. I want it free. Like manna from heaven. Else I don't want it. They can stuff it.' He raised his hands when he said 'manna' and smiled and she saw that he was delighted by the imaginary success and by his integrity and that this pleasure was spilling over into the feeling he got from sitting here with her. She put one finger on the pulse of his wrist. It was racing. 'Success,' he said again and she guessed that she herself, because of the way she looked – her rich air – had slipped the word into his mouth as priests slip in the communion wafer. 'It's no good,' he pleaded, 'if you have to sweat for it. It's like love. You wouldn't try to buy love? You can see, can't you, how the quality itself would leave it? You'd get something . . . devalued.'

'A communion wafer without the miracle?'

'We-ell . . .' The image surprised him.

On her other side the Africans were still discussing religion.

'When God puts us in the pressure-cooker,' the talker was telling the listener, 'when the period of testing comes, then the whole key is in the rudder . . .'

'But surely success isn't at all like love?' Jane argued. 'Isn't it meant to be sweated for? Isn't that the whole point?'

The man she had lived with had thought so.

Fritz laughed. His teeth were stained and he had a huge violent laugh. She liked the stain, thinking of it as earthy, more real and animal than the white teeth of the man who had been her lover.

'I can tell where you got those ideas,' Fritz challenged. 'From some guy who made it the hard way and had to convince himself he hadn't paid too high a price. He had to pretend that the sweat was part of the reward, right? Don't you see that that's crazy? You must keep each thing separate. Listen: if I paint a painting and I like it: great. Then if someone else likes it too and pays me for it that's a bonus. But I mustn't *paint* the painting to get the money.'

'Because you might fail?'

He shrugged, annoyed at her slowness, and she said, 'No, I do see – only, isn't it dangerous then to have an exhibition?'

Fritz frowned. 'Well, I suppose, strictly speaking . . .'

She laughed at his scruple. 'You're being monkish?' she cried. 'Or like a prince.'

'Why a prince?' But he was pleased.

'Because in fairy stories,' she told him, 'princes get things without working for them. A magic animal comes and offers them the thing. Or they get it by luck or a trick. No sweat.'

'Will you have dinner with me?' he asked.

'Have you any money?'

'I could get some . . . I think.' She guessed it had only now occurred to him that she would expect to eat in a decent restaurant.

'I'll pay.' She was amused by his relief.

He walked her back to her flat, talking about his hopes. Stumbling on the cobbled street, he leaned into her with his huge corpse-like teeth and she thought: they'll fall out of his skull. Like dice they must rattle in the hollow of his mouth. Passing a shop-window mirror, she saw the pair of them and how mismatched they were. But he seemed unaware of this. His voice was confident and it was clear that he believed she had recognized in him a special, secret worth.

They passed posters for tenants' leagues, workers' groups, a football club. These urged solidarity. *Vivent les Verts! Locataires, unissez-vous!* It was as though all Paris were forming factions and people propping each other up like stumbling winos. 'Ulrike Meinhof,' shrieked a yard-high graffito, 'has been murdered.' Passion implored response. A poster showed naked men being tortured in Uruguay. The caption rebuked the French for importing fruit from a state which treated citizens like this. 'We eat their nectarines', it blazoned and the effect was to make viewers feel as though they had been eating the flesh so vulnerably displayed. Jane noted with discomfort that the blown-up photographs were of young, attractive, naked males and that her first response had been the wrong one.

The man beside her had a hand on her shoulder and she felt he might march her off to behind some barricade from which she would not be let emerge. He was a primitive kind of man unused to social play.

At the door of her flat she said, 'I won't ask you in. I have things to do.'

Upstairs the phone was ringing. It was her former lover calling from America. 'Sweetie,' he said in a voice which seemed in the room with her. 'Isn't it time you pulled yourself together? How long more do you intend staying in Paris? What are you doing there? What are you doing with your life?'

'I've got a job in a gallery.'

'You're too old for Left-Bank drifting. Are they paying you?'

She remembered his shrewd eye and how his pinstripe suits reminded her of ruled pages in an account book. His shirt cuffs and collar emerged like margins from the dark jackets, and the hairs on his wrists suggested areas of his body which looked hygienically bestial in bed. His fastidiousness evoked filth as a gauze mask might germs.

'I told you,' she said, 'I'm not coming back.'

'Your mother is worried,' he remarked. 'What shall I tell her?'

She felt a rush of anger and at the same time fear that this could be a sign of faltering will. 'You crush me,' she accused. 'You define me. I am nobody while I am with you.'

'Women's lib chat,' he derided. 'You've picked that up like a parrot. Is it better to let *them* define you?'

'Ah,' she lamented, 'you don't even believe I can have a mind of my own.'

She went back to the café to wait for Fritz and it seemed to her that it was full of weak, worried men. She liked that. Her lover had been so successful that there had been no point in her doing anything while she stayed with him. He earned so much that anything she did was reduced to the status of a hobby. The men here were different. Dream was their dimension. They kept their shirt cuffs concealed and talked of ways to cheat or save. She guessed that they must have first come to Paris seeking some principle of order which it had represented to them. They must have hoped to intellectually dominate or even change the city's system. Now they were content merely to slide round it, surviving by stealth and entering cinemas and métro stations by back ways as a cockroach enters houses by their plumbing. Turning former principles on their heads, they flattered themselves that theirs was a heroic rejection of established values. When a waiter brought her drink the man at the next table tapped her elbow.

'Another time,' he advised, 'ask for a round glass. The fluted ones hold less.' He closed an eye.

'Thank you,' said Jane. Then: 'Why do you stay in Paris?'

The man looked surprised. 'It's where I live.'

This man was organizing a local tenants' strike. There was to be a meeting later that evening in the café and earlier she had heard him plan strategy with excitement. He was from Ohio.

'Oh,' he said defensively, 'maybe it's not of world-shaking importance. But it's worth doing. I enjoy it. *C'est marrant.*'

Jane guessed that she must have looked at him with her former lover's unsettling stare. It was a trick she had picked up. The strike-leader looked unsettled. He went on explaining and she dropped her eyes.

At dinner she told the painter, 'I'm not interested in sex, you know. It's not what I'm after.'

'Eat your shishkebabs,' he advised. 'Stop trying to tie now to another time, to an aim, a hope. Happiness is now. It's shish-kebabs.'

'Let me ask you,' she said, 'are you tying now to what you think we might be doing later? Are you planning on making love?'

'If it happens it'll be good.'

'It won't happen,' she told him. 'I've got a vaginal disorder of nervous origin and I can't make love.'

'Well don't be so triumphant.'

'You mind, don't you,' she accused. 'You did have a plan?'

'Yes,' he admitted in the end. 'I mind.'

Later they went back to the café and watched the winos go through their mime, begging, gargling fire, insulting drinkers who wouldn't pay. Fritz grew morose. When he leaned towards her she smelled unwashed clothes. As he drank, his resentment swelled. Critics and gallery owners drew his rage. It occurred to her that if success were to strike him, diving like a vulture from the heaven he imagined intent on scowling down at him, this would be the ultimate affront.

'I'm not one of your mini-failures!' he shouted all of a sudden. 'Nope. When I fail I do it right. If I fall off the tight-rope I do it when the safety-net holders are on their tea-break. You kids know nothing.' He looked around the café with a grin which was half hostile yet seductive too. He wanted them to listen.

But the tenants' committee was intent on its affairs at the other end of the *terrasse* and the tables in between were filled with French. Fritz had to be content with Jane. 'I'm a grade-A failure,' he told her. 'I should do what old ballet-stars do and open a school. Deliver diplomas. Suicide excluded. Your true failure muffs even that. He injures himself hideously but survives.'

'Are you thinking of your exhibition?' Jane asked.

'I won't talk about that,' he said. 'I don't give a damn about that. Maybe I won't even go through with it.'

'Of course failing with *you*,' he said, 'was no challenge. I mean how could I win? Anyone can see you're self-absorbed and on the make. I should try with one of the wino women. Now if I fail with one of them I really score, don't I? Watch me.'

Drunkenly or with pretended drunkenness, he walked into the middle of the square, the winos' territory, where he began talking to a female drunk. Jane saw him produce a hip-flask and offer it around. The winos drank ceremonially.

Jane left.

For some days she did not go back to the café. She tried to find a job. But she felt too old to accept a beginner's wage and she had no skills. Her lover rang again.

'Your mother wants your number,' he said. 'Shall I give it to her?'

'No.'

Eventually she went round to look at Fritz's exhibition.

'He's gone to lunch,' the girl at the desk greeted her. 'You're Jane, aren't you? He thought you'd have come sooner. You may as well take over. I'm fed up here. There's nothing to do. He brought everyone he knew the first day.'

Jane looked at the signatures in the visitors' book.

'They're imaginary,' the girl told her. 'I wrote them in so he wouldn't feel so bad. You may as well add some.'

'I thought he didn't care about success?'

'You must be joking?' The girl stood stuffing possessions into a shoulder bag. 'Lock the door,' she said, 'if you go out. There's a bar at the corner serves sandwiches.'

Jane had a look at the paintings. They were made up of criss-crossed lines. She examined the names in the visitors' book and felt her eyes dull with boredom. She shook her head and a painting across from her fell into focus so that she saw it was not abstract after all. The crosshatching formed a design. A darkness was a woman's vulva and slopes rising from it must be thighs or wings. They churned; their substance quailed. Serrated edges represented gashed flesh. Pinions thrust around it in punishing embrace. It was Leda and the swan but the bird was made of metal: a robot. It held Leda's neck in the noose of its own and its webbed feet oozed with the slime of rivers. Moist brush strokes smudged the limbs, reducing them to mud tracts and the pubic growth to sedge. Hair, fanning across the canvas, became algae and the swan threshed in a lone dream of sexual congress on an empty delta. Metamorphosed, the girl had got away. A twitch of the viewer's head and the swan too was gone, absorbed in an imbrication of triangles.

Jane felt excited. Response to the canvas came from a part of herself which had not had a chance to come to life before. It was a force which had been unable to emerge because she had no skill to channel it.

She felt like a deaf singer who, on being cured, hears her own voice for the first time. Was such a thing possible?

The patterns wavered. Fritz's perceptions lacked courage. He needed someone to reassure and organize him. She screwed up her eyes seeking the biological soup, the swan's emerging wing, the dank, vaginal secretions of its victim. Had Fritz intended these? Was she playing Rorschach games with his designs? Impossible to tell but the canvas had a wriggling vigour which enthralled the eye. She looked at his other paintings and here too saw hints of myth. The child's sandbox side to his work moved her. She had not wanted a man.

'I'm not going to leave you for another man,' she had told her lover. 'I'm going to find *myself*.' When she found she had contracted a vaginal illness she had felt reassured, taking this as a sign that her body was abetting her and she had not bothered to see a doctor. But sex with Fritz would be different to the sensual play she had renounced. It could only be a consubstantiation of something already achieved on a more important level. His art completed her. She would be midwife to his art. Quite suddenly she knew she had a receptive talent. More: she had creative vision, would tell him how to paint. They would form a team, producing art not babies and she would explain their conceptions to the world. She would also sell them. From her former lover she had learned the importance of self-promotion. How necessary it was. Poor Fritz had no idea.

She waited for him with impatience.

'Fritz,' she greeted him when he came, 'you've sold nothing. Don't bother looking at the visitors' book. Those names are phony. That girl wrote them in. Give it to me.' She closed it. 'As I said, you've sold nothing, but you can make an acquisition. Look.'

She had taken one of the red spots by which galleries indicate that a painting has been sold and stuck it on her forehead like an Indian woman's caste mark.

Fritz stared. His mind, she saw, was on the book with the invented signatures – perhaps she should not have told him about them? – and he did not catch her drift.

Jane pointed to the red spot. 'I'm yours,' she told him, 'if you want me. You said,' she reminded, 'that you wouldn't sweat for things you wanted. You did say that, didn't you? Well, here I am.' She waited. 'No strings attached. If you want me, that is.' His slowness was astonishing but the flirtatiousness in her voice seemed unworthy. She tried for a flat tone. 'Isn't that the way you like things?' she asked seriously. 'Total. Immediate. Now, if you like.' She was beginning to feel like an auctioneer running out of voice.

'Why?'

She waved at his canvases. 'I think you're a great painter.'

'You're having me on?'

'No.' Jane flung out her arms.

He flung himself into them. Together, stumbling like winos, they made for and locked the gallery door. They made love on the carpet. The vaginal malady proved no deterrent, although penetration hurt. Jane imagined Fritz as the swan-god in his painting, a metallic Zeus ploughing her sick marshes. The image reconciled her to his smell which was of the sort one might get in a hamper of soiled laundry. She wondered if he had been sleeping with the wino women and whether she herself was now communing at a remove with the sexual dregs of Paris. Well there was glamour in diving to the depths. And nerve. She was impressed by her own enterprise.

'Plato . . .' she panted as Fritz pumped into her. She told him how men and women could be cerebrally supplementary. 'You need someone to believe in you,' she explained, 'your work lacks assurance.'

He didn't lack it here on the gallery floor, though she became fuzzily aware that perhaps he should have. His shape was strange to her. Probably café food and sitting in cafés had lowered ballast to his belly for it was as solidly large as a pregnant woman's.

'Afraid I've got a *brioche*,' he used the French understatement, amiably patting it, oddly unaware for a visual man how this gross evidence told against him.

Like a glutton's in a Last Judgment painting, his sin ballooned and manifested corporeality where Jane had been seeking spirit. She was ready to transcend flesh – but could this packed and substantive stuff be transcended? Whereas communion wafers were the frailest form of bread, this matter rose yeastily like a wave gone solid, a buttress wall of lard. Before rising from an embrace which had begun in hallucination, she knew she had made a mistake. His painting might delight. His body didn't. The pain in her vagina had only sharpened her sense of mission, focusing the sacrificial nature of their joining. But fleshiness is flesh's enemy and Jane, who had been trying to get nearer, felt further. Wrestling with the wads of matter separating her from Fritz – where *was* he? was this irrelevant stuff he? – she saw and set about trying to mask failure. *He must not know.* Effortfully, she lashed her bony back about the floor, miming delight and striving to provide a satisfactory memory of what – she knew, panted, bravely lashed – would be a unique occasion. First and last. Her vagina had gone dry. She smuggled down some saliva, hoping he hadn't seen. But now, once she had allowed herself to reflect at all, disgust began to gain. Fritz's body seemed decayed. How could she have forgotten those teeth? They bore down on her like the prongs of an old hay rake. What if one, loosened by kissing, were to fall into her own mouth? She imagined it on her tongue, alien and dry like an old acid drop, or sliding down her throat to choke her. She was going to have to deny her promises and take herself back. How do this gracefully?

'Is there a bathroom?'

'I think so.' Fritz adjusted an unreliable fly zipper and leaned to plant a kiss on her forehead. Had he too been disappointed? She prayed he had.

She bolted into an inadequate *cabinet de toilette* where she washed his smell off as much of herself as might be accommodated by the basin and bidet. She longed to put her clothes in an incinerator, jump into a cleansing ocean, steam herself in a Turkish bath. But feeling this, she felt the more bound to Fritz, since the more undesirable he was the more her rejection must damage him. Must it? Might he not be unaware of his own shortcomings? No, the painting was surely a statement of self-disgust. And how odd that she had relished those same oozy danknesses on canvas, those premonitions of death, rot and final, unfastidious human joinings. But then art was not life. It was a surrogate, a ritual warding-off. Like religion, it came between you and a homicidal reality. Fritz had warned her to keep things separate but she had not understood. Well, clearly, she was not the critic and connoisseur she had supposed. She would be no use to Fritz at all.

Returning to the front of the gallery, she peeled the red spot which spelled 'sold' from her forehead and stuck it on the corner of the Leda painting.

'I'm buying that,' she told Fritz. 'Your first sale.'

Then she left.

'I have to go,' she said. 'No, you can't see me home. I'll get a taxi. I'm late already. No time to explain. Yes, of course, ring me any time you like. Not tonight though. I'll be away. In the country. Sorry. Bye.'

After that she dodged him. What else could she do? Say?

What she did say – in a note – was that he must forget her. It had been beautiful but she didn't want to see him again. She was going through changes. It was a difficult time in her life. She would cherish his painting and memory. Goodbye.

He tried to ring her. He called to the door. Her cleaning woman – now furnished with a set of splendid smiling teeth supplied by the Sécurité Sociale – told him that Madame was out, away, gone, sick, unavailable. Easily, as she might have done with a cockroach, she swept him out.

He wrote to say that if Jane believed in his talent she should prove it. Her belief meant more to him than she could know. He was haunted by the parable of the buried talent, yet somehow could not get his work off the ground. He needed her. She needed him. He repeated the promises she had panted out that day on the gallery floor, adding embellishments and analyses of his own.

'Your generation of women,' he wrote, 'wasn't bred to stand alone. If you don't come to me you'll go back to your sugar daddy. You can't make it by yourself. It would take you years to develop a skill. But you have vision. You and I could be a team. I could be your mission. Many women sought just that sort of outlet in the past. Women as sensitive as you. It takes a special talent to help a man with his art. You have it . . .'

She didn't finish the letter. Fritz was obviously trying to con her, she decided, and her guilt and pity for him vanished. Artists, she remembered now, had always tended to exploit women. She'd been lucky to escape his trap.

When her old lover rang she let him, slowly, persuade her to return to him.

'You're not bred for fighting in the market place,' he told her, 'or inching your way up the ladder. Your place is at the top. I can put you there.'

'I've bought a painting,' she told him.

'I'm sure it's good. You have a talent for buying. You have an eye. You're a home-maker.'

'I'd rather be a dealer,' she argued, her mind filling with new projects. 'If I *have* got an eye . . .'

'Well come back home here,' he advised, 'where you've got contacts.'

'We'll discuss it,' she warned. 'I'm serious.'

'Sure.'

'People who despise dealers are *crass*!' She was arguing with the ghost of Fritz. 'Did you know,' she harangued her lover, 'that Leonardo da Vinci put painting above sculpture because it was less physical, because of the brutish effort involved in hacking marble or casting bronze?'

'You can tell me about it when you get here.'

'But painting is physical too. You muck dirt around on a canvas like, I don't know, a kid playing with faeces. That might be how it got started.'

'Maybe. Listen,' her lover sounded wary, 'let me know your flight number as soon as you're booked.'

'God, when he was creating,' Jane told him, 'said "let there be light" and there was. It was all done with an idea, you see. With a word. Later he looked at what he'd done and saw that it was good. Just like a dealer who thinks up projects, gets other people to do the donkey work, then promotes the product. *He's* the real creator. Anyway that's the sort of dealer I have in mind to be if you back me.'

'The power behind the easel?'

'Right.'

'OK, Mrs God. I'll start making straight the paths. Now when may we expect a visitation?'

'Soon.'

She went round to the gallery to arrange to have Fritz's painting shipped to the States. The same girl was there.

'I don't know the procedure,' the girl told her. 'He didn't sell any others. And he's in hospital. Didn't you know? He started gargling methylated spirits the other night. You know the winos' trick? He set fire to it but it burned his throat. I gather it's a horrible business. It seems he was drunk and in despair about some woman who'd led him on. He's very naive, Fritz. Well, I'll ask the gallery owners to see about your painting. OK?'

'Right,' said Jane and gave the girl her American address.

'I'm sorry about Fritz,' she remarked. 'The guy couldn't organize reality at all, could he? I suppose he'll be able to go on painting? Good thing he wasn't a singer.'

Diego

Diego? He hasn't been in touch? Well, but that's his way, isn't it? He can just drop out of sight, then come back later, bubbling with good humour and gifts. He's so good-natured one has to forgive him. Of course he trades on that. I did see him recently, as it happens. Mmm. About two weeks ago and a funny thing happened then – funny things do when one is with him, don't you find? Or maybe it's he who makes them seem funny because he enjoys a laugh so much. He was giving me a lift home to have dinner with his wife and Mercedes, the little girl. Yes, she's ten now and bright as a button, a bit spoilt I'm afraid. Well, you'd expect Diego to spoil a daughter, wouldn't you? Of course he's in love with her and I must say she is a lovely creature. What was I going to tell you? Oh, about the supermarket. Well, Marie had asked him to stop and pick up some mangoes – you've never met *her*, have you? Am I putting my foot in it? Sorry. I know you're much older friends of Diego's than I am – but that's just the trouble, isn't it? You belong to the days when he was with Michèle and he has never felt able to present friends from those years to Marie. It's his delicacy. Another husband wouldn't give a damn. Hard on old friends. But you know what he says: 'How can I tell my wife "Here are my friends, X and Y, whom I've known for ten years but never brought home until now"?' In a way you can see his point. He neglected Marie awfully during all that time. Excluded her from his social life. You'd be a reminder of his bad behaviour. It would be different if they'd gone through with the divorce. His good nature prevented that. He couldn't bring himself to leave her and now he can't bring himself to leave Michèle, and so someone's always getting the short end of the stick.

I was telling you about the mangoes. Well, we went into the

market to get them and it was one of those places in the *banlieue* where they weren't used to selling exotic fruit. Nobody knew the price and a girl was sent off with the ones Diego had picked to try and find the manager. Then she got waylaid or went to the phone and didn't come back. The woman at the check-out shouted on the intercom, *'Où sont les mangues de Monsieur?'* At this, Diego began to fall about laughing and then everyone in the shop began to see the thing as a gag. They began shouting at each other: 'His what?' – 'His mangoes!' – 'Lost his mangoes, has he? Oh that must be painful!' – 'What? Mangoes? Oh, unmentionable!' And so forth. It was pretty mindless and any other customer might have been annoyed, but not Diego. He was delighted. 'They come from my country,' he told the girl and when he did I noticed that he *looks* like a mango: reddish and yellowish and a touch wizened. 'I'm half Red Indian,' he told her and it was obvious that if his mangoes hadn't turned up just then in a great burst of hilarity, he would have started getting off with her. He has a great way with him and he knows how to take the French. He keeps just that little touch of foreignness while speaking very racy Parisian and knowing everything there is to know about life here. They love that. He loves their ways and that makes them able to feel they can love his.

When we got back into the car, he started telling me of how once, years ago, when he first met Michèle, he was walking through the old Halles market, with her on one arm and Marie on the other, on their way to dine at an oyster bar, and one of those hefty lorry-drivers who used to bring in loads of produce began pointing at tiny Diego walking between these two splendid, *plantureuses* women – they looked like assemblages of melons, according to Diego – and, pretending to wipe his brow, raised his cap and roared: 'What a constitution?' *Quelle santé!* It was like the mango joke. Diego attracts such comments. When he told me the story, I got the idea that *that* could have been what started off his affaire with Michèle.

Because dear old Diego *is* a bit of a *macho*, isn't he, in the nicest possible way? *'Moi, j'aime la femme,'* he says. Awfully Latin! It sounds impossible in English. I mean you can't say it really: 'I love woman' sounds absurd. And if you say 'women' in the plural it sounds cheap. But what he means is the essence of woman, something he sees in every woman, even in his mother and, of course, especially in little Mercedes, right from the moment she was born. 'She was a woman,' he'll tell you – well, he probably *has* told you. He talks about her all the time. 'From the moment she was born she was a woman, a coquette, a flirt.'

As I was saying, he has spoilt her a bit – I tell a lie, he has spoilt her a great deal. In fact something happened later that evening which pointed up the dangers of this and was really quite upsetting. I don't know whether Diego will draw the lesson from it.

You haven't met Mercedes either, have you? You'd really have to see her to understand. You see, in a way, Diego is right. She *is* remarkably bright and perfectly bilingual because of his having always spoken Spanish to her. She *is* like a coquettish little princess stepped out of a canvas by Goya or Velázquez. This is partly because of her clothes which come from boutiques on the Faubourg Saint Honoré. Ridiculous clothes: hand-tucked muslin, silk, embroidered suede. I don't know who they were intended for, but Diego buys them. He buys her exactly the same sort of thing as he used to buy Michèle, and there is Marie in her denims with a daughter wearing a mink jacket at the age of ten. I don't know whether she approves or not. Their relationship is odd. Well, most marriages seem that way to me. What do I know of yours, for instance? Married people always strike me as treating each other a bit like bonsai trees. They nip and clip and train each other into odd, accommodating shapes, then sometimes complain about the result. Or one partner can go to endless lengths of patience with the other and then be obdurate about some trifling thing. It's a mystery. I watch with interest. I think you're all a dying species but fun to watch – like some product of a very ancient, constricting, complex civilization. Perhaps that's why I'm a gossip? As a feminist, I am in the same position as the Jesuits who watched and noted down the ways of the old Amerindians while planning to destroy them.

Diego claims sometimes to be part Amerindian. Maybe he is. Some of them used to cut out their victims' hearts with stone knives, used they not? I'm not sure whether *he* may not have blood on his hands. Metaphorical blood. After all, he's a member of the oligarchy of that repressive regime. It's true that he has been twenty-five years in Paris, reads the left-wing press and has picked up a radical vocabulary – but where does his money come from? Well, one doesn't probe but one can't help wondering. Another complexity. The troubling thing about sexists and members of old, blood-sodden castes is that they can be so delicate in their sensibilities and this does throw one. I keep meeting people like that here in Paris. It seems to draw them as honey draws wasps. Am I being the Protestant spinster now? Forthright and angular and killing the thing I love as I lean over it with my frosty breath? In delighted disapproval? In disapproving delight. I mustn't kill this little story which I'm working my way round to telling you. It's about Mercedes and Michèle's dog. Yes, but first, have you got the background clear in your minds? Diego is so jokey and jolly and often – to be frank – drunk, that you mightn't. *Your* dealings with him were always social, weren't they? You'd meet in some smart night club or restaurant and, I suppose, dance till dawn with money no object and champagne flowing. That's how I imagine it – how Diego's led me to imagine it. Am I wrong? No? Good. Well, but, you see, that's only one side of Diego: the Don Diego swaggering side. There's also the plainer homebody. Did you know that Diego is simply the Spanish for James? I didn't either. Think of him as 'Jim' or 'Jacques' coming home in the dishwater-dawn light from those evenings to the surburban house where he'd parked Marie and the child.

Marie's *my* friend, by the way. I knew her before I did him. She had gone back to university to study law and we met in a feminist student group. Well, what would you have her do all those years while he used the house as a launching pad for his flights of jollification? He brought home the minimum cash – just like any working-class male taking half the budget for his pleasures. She could have left. She didn't. *There's* an area of motives which one cannot hope to map. *He* could have left and didn't. There's one I *can* map for you. He met Michèle through Marie. In those days she had prettier friends. I do occasionally wonder whether *I* was chosen as being unthreatening? No, no need to protest. I'm trying for accuracy. I like to take hold of as many elements in a situation as I can and I've admitted that Diego/Jim fascinates me. He is the Male Chauvinist Pig or Phallocrate seen close up, as I rarely get a chance to see the beast, and I do see his charm. It is his weapon and, when I say I see it, I really mean that I feel him seeing the woman in me. Men don't, very often. That's what I mean about Diego's *amour pour la femme* being non-sexist or sexist in such an all-embracing way that it gets close to universal love. He loves half humanity, half the human race, regardless of age, looks or health. Of course he is *also* a sex-snob and wants to be seen with a girl who does him credit – Michèle. That's the social side of him. But he responds to femininity wherever he finds it: in his mother, an old beggar woman, me. He's inescapably kind.

Why didn't he divorce, you ask? Kindness again. Really. He had fallen in love with Michèle: a tempestuous passion, I gather. They were swept off by it simultaneously, like a pair of flint stones knocking sparks off each other, like two salamanders sizzling in unison – he tells me about it when Marie's in the kitchen. He has to tell someone. It was his big experience and he made a mess of it and is still shocked at himself, yet can't see how he could have done other than he did. What he did was this: he proposed marriage to Michèle, was accepted and, brimful of bliss, looked at poor, blissless Marie and thought how lonely she must be and that he must do something for her. Now here is the part that touches me. He didn't think in terms of money, as most men would have. He thought in terms of love. He wanted her to have someone to love when he had gone off with Michèle and decided that *he* had better be the one to provide her with a love-object. Can you guess the next move? He made her pregnant. The noble sexist wanted to leave her with a child. Imagine Michèle's fury. She thought that he had got cold feet about marrying *her* and had cooked up this pretext for backing out. He assured her that he did very much want to marry her but that now he must stay with Marie until the baby was born so that it should be legitimate.

The baby, of course, was Mercedes and he fell in love with *her* at first sight, at first sound, at first touch. He was totally potty about her, obsessed and *at the same time* he was painfully in love with an estranged and furious Michèle on whom he showered guilty, cajoling gifts, spoiling and courting her and putting up with every caprice in an effort to earn back the total love which he had forfeited – she kept telling him – by his sexual treachery.

Those were the years when you knew him – the champagne and dancing years. He and Michèle had not got married and so their relationship became one long, festive courtship and she, from what he says, responded as someone who's fussed over for years might well be tempted to respond: she became a bit of a bitch. She brought boys home to the flat where he kept her like a queen, stood him up, tormented him and then, between lovers, just often enough to keep him hot for her, became as loving and playful as they had been in the early days. She was his *princesse lointaine*, radiant with the gleam of loss and old hope and he was romantic about her and probably happier than he admits with the arrangement which kept his loins on fire and fixed his wandering attention on her in whom he was able to find all women: the wife she should have become, the fickle tormentor she had become, his wronged great love and familiar old friend, his Donna Elvira and his spendthrift, nightclub succubus. She was all women except one and that one, to be sure, was Mercedes, the little girl who was growing up in an empty, half-furnished suburban house with a mother who was busy getting her law degree and a father who swept in from time to time with presents from Hamleys and Fouquets and organdie dresses and teddy bears twice her size which made her cry. Every penny he had went on Michèle and Mercedes. I remember that house when it hadn't a lamp or a table because Marie was damned if she'd spend *her* money on it and he was so rarely there that he never noticed what it did or didn't have apart from the Aladdin's Cave nursery in which Mercedes was happy while she was small. Later, at the ages of six and seven and eight, as she began to invite in her friends, she began to colonize the rest of the house and, as she did, he began to furnish it for her. Michèle's share of his budget shrank as Mercedes's grew. Shares in his time fluctuated too. He spent more of it at home; friends like you began to see less of him and Michèle had to start finding herself new escorts, not from bitchery but from need. But he would never abandon her completely. He had wasted her marriageable years and now he felt towards her the guilt he had once felt towards Marie. But what can he do? He's not Christ. He cannot divide up and distribute his body and blood.

He was telling me all this that night on the drive out from Paris and he got so upset that at one stage he stopped the car and walked into a hotel where we had a drink. This made us late for dinner, but Marie, of course, never complains. Who did complain was

Mercedes. It was past her bed-time and she was irritable and sleepy when we arrived. She had waited up because she wanted to have a mango and, besides, Diego had promised her some small present. Right away she started being whingey and angry with me whom she blamed for keeping her Daddy late. Diego was amused, as he is by all Mercedes's caprices, and kept saying, 'She's jealous, you know!' As though that were something to be proud of! 'She's very possessive.'

There was a dog in the house, Michèle's silver poodle – perhaps you know it? – Rinaldino, a rather highly-strung creature which Marie and Mercedes had been told was mine. Michèle had asked Diego to keep it for her because she was going on a cruise and it pines if left in a kennel. Diego can never say 'no' to Michèle, and so a story was concocted about my flat being painted and how I had had to move to a hotel where I couldn't take my new dog. All this because of Diego's not wanting his wife to know that she was being asked to house his mistress's dog. Surprisingly, the plan had worked up to now and Rinaldino had been three weeks at Diego's. Mercedes was mad about him and everyone had been pleased about that. This evening, however, she suddenly announced that from now on the dog was hers. She wasn't giving him back. She just wasn't. So there. The dog loved her, she claimed and, besides, she had told her friends it was hers and didn't want to be made to look a liar. She said all this in her grown-up way: half playful, half testing and I couldn't help having the old-fashioned notion that what she really wanted, deep down, was to be told 'no'. That used to be said, remember, when *we* were children. It was thought that children needed to know the limits of their possibilities.

Anyway, she kept on and Diego wouldn't contradict her and neither did Marie. I kept my mouth shut. It's not my business if Diego spoils his daughter as he spoils his mistress so, even though the dog was supposed to be mine, I didn't react when Mercedes started clamouring for a promise that Dino, as she had rechristened Rinaldino, should never leave. She would not go to bed till she got it, she said. It was obvious that she was trying to provoke me, but I pretended not to notice. Poor child, it's not her fault if she is the way she is.

'Dino likes me better than he likes you,' she told me.

'Why wouldn't he like you?' I asked. 'You're a good girl, aren't you?'

'He likes me whether I'm good or not. He likes me even when I hurt him.'

I can't remember what I said to that and doubt if it mattered. She had taken against me and the next thing she did was to start twisting the dog's ears.

'See,' she said. 'Even when I do this, he likes me. He likes me because he's mine. I'm his Mummy.'

Then she began to cuddle the animal in that way that children do if they're not stopped. She tied a napkin under its chin, half choking it, and held it as if it were a baby, bending its spine and pretending to rock it to sleep.

'Mine, mine, mine,' she crooned.

I had an odd sensation as I watched. What struck me was that in a way the dog was *Michèle's* baby, her substitute for the family she might have had if Mercedes had not been born. And now, here was Mercedes trying to steal even that from her. I found myself wondering whether some instinct was making her do it. An intuition? The thought was absurd but I let myself play with it to keep my mind off what the brat was doing to little Rinaldino. The French *are* insensitive about animals and Marie seemed indifferent. She often goes into a sort of passive trance when Diego is around and he, of course, has no feeling for creatures at all. Maybe I was showing my discomfort in spite of myself? I can't be sure. Anyway, the little beast – I'm talking about Mercedes – began to pull Rinaldino's whiskers and it was all I could do to keep myself from slapping her. I was on the point of warning her that she might get bitten when she gave a shriek and threw the dog violently across the room. For a moment I thought she might have broken its back, but no, it got up and scuttled under the sofa. That, it turned out, was good canine thinking.

It had bitten her cheek. Not deeply, but it had drawn blood.

Well, the scene after that was beyond description, unbelievable. It literally took my breath away: hysteria, screams, foot-stamping, hand-wringing – all the things you think real people never do, they did. And no initiative at all. *I* had to take charge and clean the child's cheek and put disinfectant on it. You'd think I'd cut off her head from the way she carried on. Diego was crying. Marie was tight-lipped and kept clenching her fists as though she was about to explode.

'Look,' I told them, 'it's a scratch. It's nothing. She'd have got worse from a bramble bush. Just *look*,' I kept insisting.

But they wouldn't. Not really. They kept exclaiming and averting their faces and clapping their hands over their eyes. They wanted their drama and were working each other up, so that when Mercedes shouted, 'I want the dog killed. Right now. It doesn't like me. It doesn't love me. It must be killed!' I realized that the adults were half ready to go along with the idea. Diego was completely out of his mind.

'Supposing it has rabies?' he whispered to me.

'It's been inoculated,' I told him.

'Are you sure?'

'Of course I am. It's on its name tag. Look. With the date.'

'I want it killed now! Here. Now. It doesn't love me. It's a bad dog,' screamed Mercedes.

'It's my dog,' I told her. 'You can't kill my dog.'

She began to kick me then. Hard. I still have bruised shins. She carried on as if she had rabies herself and her mother had to pull her off me and take her to bed.

'I want it killed!' She was screaming and scratching and biting as they went through the door. Later, I heard her still at it in her bedroom.

Diego looked distraught. He said he had heard of dogs which were rabid in spite of having been inoculated. Was I *sure* it had been inoculated? What did a name tag prove after all? It struck me then that he had either forgotten that the dog was not mine or was trying to persuade himself that it was. We were alone together now but he avoided mentioning Michèle's name. Maybe he felt that some sin of his was coming to the fore and demanding a blood sacrifice? He kept pouring whisky and drinking it down fast. At one point he went into the kitchen and looked at the rack of knives.

Well, you can never tell how much that sort of thing is theatre, can you? I mean that theatre can spill into life if people work themselves up enough. Maybe he was seeing himself as an Amerindian priest? I don't mind telling you that I began to get scared.

The thing was taking on odd dimensions as he got drunker and guiltier and the screams ebbed and started up again in the bedroom. Rinaldino, very sensibly, stayed right where he was under the sofa and that affected me more than anything. After all, dogs do pick up bad vibrations, don't they? Anyway, the outcome was that when Diego went into the lavatory I phoned a taxi, took the dog and left. I was convinced that by now he wasn't seeing the dog as a dog at all and that if I hadn't got it out of the house he would have ended up killing it – or worse.

Marie wouldn't have interfered. Even if she'd been standing beside him she wouldn't. I'm sure of that. They're extraordinary that way. I keep thinking of them now. Each is so intelligent and kind and – I want to say 'ordinary', when they're on their own. Normal? But let a scene start and you'd think you were dealing with members of the House of Atreus. Marie's passivity has started to seem sinister to me. I've started dreaming of that evening and it's become deformed in my memory. Sometimes it seems to me that she was the silent puppet-mistress pulling the strings and that even I was one of the puppets. Even the dog. Well, certainly the dog. Maybe it's self-referential to bring myself in? But I've started worrying whether Marie as well as Mercedes sees me as an intrusive female. 'She's jealous,' Diego told me that evening and laughed. He could have meant his wife. Could he? I'm only his confidante but Marie might dislike that, mightn't she? It's very unhealthy on my part to dwell on the thing and it would be absurd for me to have a crush on a man like Diego and I hope nobody thinks this is the case. In my more sober moments I know that any bad feeling that came my way that evening was really directed through me at Michèle. I was her stand-in. After all, I'd pretended to own her dog. But somehow, emotion sticks. I feel a little as though mud had been thrown at me and that I can't quite clean it off.